Jack Vance
Bird Isle

Jack Vance

Bird Isle

John H. Vance

Spatterlight Press Signature Series, Volume 16

Published by Spatterlight Press

Cover art by Howard Kistler

ISBN 978-1-61947-147-4

Spatterlight Press LLC

Spatterlight
P R E S S
340 S. Lemon Ave #1916
Walnut, CA 91789

www.jackvance.com

Jack Vance
Bird Isle

CHAPTER I

SUNLIGHT SPARKLED ON THE WATER; the surf rushing up Bird Island beach glistened an aching white. Along the horizon a gray midge of a steamer eased south, the intervening sea as blue as cobalt. The old gray planks of the hotel veranda soaked up the sun, giving off the pleasant incense of hot weathered wood. From the beach came the smell of salt water, kelp; from the hills behind the hotel drifted the fragrance of heather, sage, verbena, cedar.

Coves yawned, flexed his arms, and glanced approvingly down the front of the hotel. What if the paint was peeling? When times got better, new paint might — or might not — be applied, depending on how Coves felt at the moment. In the meantime the old place had atmosphere.

The door from the lobby opened and one of the regular guests, Mrs. Lukens, came hobbling out. This was Mrs. Lukens' favorite chair in which he sat. Oh, well, thought Coves — one of the minor inconveniences of operating a resort hotel. He prepared to rise.

Rexie, the hotel cat, who lay sprawled across the veranda enjoying the sunshine, cried out in anguish, and Mrs. Lukens fell creaking to the worn rag rug.

Coves leaped forward and assisted the groaning woman to a chair.

"Mr. Coves," she gasped, "I don't know what this place is coming to. It's a mortal risk staying here. This morning I caught my heel in the carpet on the stair and nearly fell, and the hot-water tap pinches my hand every time I turn it — and there's never any hot water —"

"First thing I'll attend to."

"— and that cat everywhere so that it's an ordeal walking across the floor..."

Mrs. Lukens fell quiet, and Coves went to his desk in the dim lobby.

Afternoon fog creeping in from the ocean blocked out the sun. Coves looked around the lobby. Dingy place. Rickety furnishings. He kept the few guests he did only because his rates were low. *Quiet old-fashioned atmosphere, no expensive extras* — so read the modest advertisement he ran in the *San Francisco Chronicle* twice a month.

A vision came before his eyes, the advertisement as it should have read: *Gayety, laughter, romance, in an atmosphere of sumptuous luxury! Exquisite appointments, continental cuisine, the most fashionable watering place this side of Biarritz! Thrill to the glamour of a vacation at exciting Bird Island Hotel!*

Coves, contrasting the image with the fact, sighed. Since many of his guests supported temperance societies, Coves dared not push the sale of whisky. And when, occasionally, someone young and lively wandered in, they found nothing to entertain them. Mrs. Lukens, Mr. Bates, Miss Throop, and Mrs. Arly preempted the lobby with a nightly rubber of whist, and scowled at distracting sounds — especially dance music. It was a vicious circle, thought Coves.

The door opened, and Al Carper, who operated the launch to Monterey, lounged in. Carper was grotesque and gangling, with eyes almost adjoining across the big shell of his nose.

"Hi there, Coves," said Carper. "Looks like you lost your last friend."

Coves shook his head. "This is a nerve-wracking business, Al. Sometimes I don't think it's worth the effort."

"Well," said Carper, helping himself to a toothpick, "seems like everybody's got his headache. I got mine and it's a dilly. If you think you're hard-pressed, you ought to try cranking my ol' engine some cold morning. Then you'd know what grief really is."

"You don't have to please the public," said Coves. "There's a thousand things to think of, and money is so short these days."

Carper gazed around the lobby. "Funny you don't get more business. This is certainly the spot for it. Nice climate, all them trees and hills behind you, so close to Monterey and Carmel. It's an ideal spot… Finest place in the world for surf fishing."

Coves rubbed his chin. "I can't understand why the hotel isn't more popular."

"You ought to do the place over," said Carper. "Expand, renovate, bring yourself up to date."

"Expand? Why, we're barely able to pay our bills now."

"Seems to me," said Carper, "that you've got a lot of land you don't use. This is valuable property, this island. If you sold off a little of it, you'd take in enough to make something of the place. Put on a couple wings, a good bar, a swimming pool…"

"I don't think that would be wise," muttered Coves.

Carper shrugged. "You're land-poor, Coves. Why, with a few thousand bucks you could really make a landmark out of the place. Look at Del Monte. Big bands playing there every night, all them society people throwing their money around. Why, man, there's people that would go big money for a slice of land out here."

Coves pursed his lips. "Oh well…"

"Aside from the ten, twenty acres old lady Pickett runs her school on, you've got the whole island. Think of how they subdivide ashore — little bits of lots, and then they want five hundred or a thousand for 'em."

"Well, that's completely out of the question," said Coves. "If I sold, it would be in larger sections, to keep the island from being cluttered. And naturally I'd have to ask a very high price."

"That's the ticket," said Carper. "Lay it on 'em when you have the chance, grab while the grabbing's good. After all, they made it getting into you, one way or another."

Coves nodded. "I suppose you're right. I pay those tremendous taxes, and everything is so high these days…"

Coves, looking up from his desk, saw approaching across the lobby a young man with an artless and carefree expression. He wore a dark blue sweater, faded dungarees, and had an unruly thatch of brown hair. He stopped by the desk. "I'd like to speak to Mr. R. M. Coves."

"I'm Mr. Coves," said Coves.

"My name is Milo Green."

They shook hands.

"I saw your ad in the paper and thought I'd investigate. From the water the island looks beautiful. I sailed down this morning."

"You're from San Francisco?"

"Right across the bay. Sausalito."

"Very pleasant," said Coves.

"I think I'd like it better down here…Tell me, just how are you subdividing?"

Coves grimaced. "I'd hardly call it subdividing — although I suppose it amounts to that. There's quite a lot of the island I don't use, which I'd like to see in qualified hands."

Milo nodded. "Just what sections are for sale?"

Coves cleared his throat. "May I ask what your plans would be?"

"I'm what you might call an author — a writer — and I'm considering Bird Island as a place to live."

"I see," said Coves. "Of course, we'd be glad to have you on the island…I'm naturally reluctant to consider anyone who might lower the tone of the place. We want only high-class neighbors, in every respect."

"I suppose I'm high-class," said Milo.

"Oh I'm sure you are," said Coves hurriedly.

"Just what is for sale, and what — ah, is the price range?"

Coves fumbled among his ledgers and account books. "Somewhere — here it is. This is a map of Bird Island. Miss Pickett occupies this section tinted red with her school, and the blue area we'll need here at the hotel. To the north is this section marked 'One', and to the south Sections Two, Three, Four and Five. Section One is the high point up there overlooking the bay, and it's perhaps the least accessible of the five. Block Two includes part of the beach facing the mainland. That's a very nice beach, and really less exposed than this one, which gets the full force of the ocean. And it's a cleaner beach, too. I can hardly keep my beach clean. Sometimes I think we catch all the driftwood and trash in Monterey Bay here on Bird Island. We get a lot of the Japanese net floats, too."

"Japanese net floats?"

Coves indicated a dusty shelf laden with globes of rough green glass, ranging in size from a few inches up to almost a foot. "They escape from the nets of the Japanese fishermen and float clear across the Pacific Ocean. There's no beach for miles around," said Coves proudly, "that gets them as we do here on Bird Island."

"That's interesting," said Milo. "I've seen them but never realized what they were."

Coves returned to the map. "Well, Blocks Three and Four are very nice, on this knoll here to the south facing Point Lobos. Five includes this shoulder of hill, these picturesque rocks and this little cove. A lovely spot for a yachtsman."

Milo nodded. "And the prices?"

Coves flushed. "Well, Mr. Green — the prices are high. You see, I'm offering very fine property. Quite extraordinary, really... Anyway," he muttered, "Number One, ten acres, is ten thousand dollars. Number Two, ten acres, is eleven thousand. Number Three, twenty-eight acres, is twenty-eight thousand. Number Four, eighteen acres, eighteen thousand dollars. Number Five, twenty-four acres, twenty-four thousand. I'd have to have cash, of course."

Milo made an understanding gesture. "You have the property for sale, you've set a price on it. If anyone wants it enough to pay the price, you'll sell. If not, you won't, and no hard feelings."

"That's it exactly," said Coves. "That's the idea."

Milo said, "If you'd let me take your map, I'd like to look the island over, and then I'll know better what's on each section."

"Certainly," said Coves. "Possibly you'd like me to show you around?"

"Oh no," said Milo, "don't bother. I'll be back in an hour or two."

He left the lobby. Al Carper, who had been sitting in an armchair reading a newspaper, joined Coves at the desk.

"He seems pleasant," said Coves. "I hope he finds a section he likes."

Carper selected a toothpick. "Them writers is a funny bunch. I seen one a week ago in Monterey. He came through driving a station wagon filled with trashy-lookin' women. Carmel is full of 'em, you know."

Coves turned to his accounts. "Mr. Green seems a nice sort of person."

"Maybe yes, maybe no," said Carper.

CHAPTER II

MILO LEFT THE HOTEL and walked north along the beach. The noonday sun was warm on his shoulders; the ocean was dead calm, with a surface sheen like the finest blue satin. Shells gleamed underfoot and sea gulls rode overhead.

To his right a lip of compacted sand edged the beach; then, behind a terrace bearded with coarse grass, the central spine of the island rose: rocky hills overgrown with heather, gorse, genista, flowering poppies, larkspur, lupines, ice plant, tarweed. And clumped along the slopes, single-file on the ridges, the Monterey cypress grew — flailing their meager black-green foliage like flags, defying wind, ocean, mountain, sun.

A gang of jagged black rocks jutted out of the beach, and here the section Coves had reserved for the hotel ended. Above rose Section One, a rocky upland, almost a crag, connected to the central part of the island by a sway-backed ridge.

Milo veered inland, climbed over rock that was at once warm and cool. Up, up, up, until finally he stood on top the crag, the island spread below. He looked to the west, out across the Pacific — miles and miles of calm blue water, a deeper blue than the air.

He turned, looked across the bay to the mainland. To his left rose the Santa Cruz Mountains; to his right, the jut of Point Lobos and the Santa Lucia Range. Two miles east was Monterey, with houses white, yellow, blue and green, the docks and warehouses black and brown, the harbor cluttered with boats.

Turning back to the island, Milo looked down the white road of Coves' beach, past the gray box of the hotel to the rocky south cape.

He looked to the other side — and there was Miss Pickett's Fine Arts
Academy and Finishing School for Select Young Ladies — a sprawling
shape of stone, brick and redwood on an expanse of very green lawn.
A gravel road ran down to a handsome stone pier, and there was a pair
of well-kept tennis courts to the rear. The school breathed an air of
prosperity.

Milo consulted the map, traced the outline of the other Blocks: Two,
beyond the school; Three and Four dividing a low hill, a wide, sunny
heave of land; Five, the cape at the southern tip of the island.

Milo seated himself on a rock…Ten thousand dollars. No small sum.
He could buy an entire house in San Francisco, a cabin at Lake Tahoe, a
rancho in the desert, a prune orchard near Santa Clara, a chicken ranch
at Petaluma…

He rose to his feet, looked out across the ocean, down at the surf on
the rocks below. "Easy come, easy go." He turned back downhill.

Rounding the corner of the hotel, he found Coves watering a row of
potted geraniums from a crockery pitcher.

Coves set the pitcher down and turned to Milo.

"How did you like the island?"

"Very much. I like Section One especially."

Coves nodded. "A magnificent view." He wiped his hands on a hand-
kerchief. "Do you — well, do you consider the price to be out of pro-
portion?"

Milo considered. "Some people might be willing to pay you twice
the price you're asking."

"Oh no," said Coves hurriedly. "I'll be happy to get ten thousand."

"Very well," said Milo. "Here it is." And he gave Coves ten thousand-
dollar bills.

"Hello? Bird Island Hotel."

"Mr. Coves, this is Miss Pickett."

"Oh yes, Miss Pickett," said Coves. "How are you?"

"Very well, thank you. Mr. Coves, I hear that you are putting your
property up for sale. I hope that this isn't true?"

Coves cleared his throat. "Not all of it, you understand. Just those
parts of the island we don't need here at the hotel."

"I should think you'd have consulted me first, Mr. Coves. After all, I'm the person most directly affected. Heaven knows what kind of people will be overrunning the island. I have trouble enough now."

Coves was aware that Miss Pickett's dock was at once the favorite goal of young Pebble Beach yachtsmen, the favorite sunning place of Miss Pickett's charges, and the focus of Miss Pickett's sharpest surveillance. He said, "Well, Miss Pickett, I'm exercising a great deal of care in selling, and anyone who isn't completely top-notch won't be considered."

"Well, I disapprove very strongly," said Miss Pickett. "There'll be considerable depreciation in the value of my property."

"I don't see why," said Coves. "I'm only selling in large acreages."

"Suppose these new owners subdivided further?" snapped Miss Pickett. "Suppose they all do? There'd be a town out here —"

"Oh no," said Coves. "I'm inserting a clause in the deeds forbidding further subdivision for ninety-nine years."

"Mmph," snorted Miss Pickett. Then after a pause, "I suppose that my opinion won't affect you one way or another, but —"

Coves said, "I'd be glad to sell to you, Miss Pickett. That would solve both our problems."

There was an instant of tense silence. Then she said, "What is your price?"

"Altogether," said Coves, "I am hoping for ninety-one thousand dollars."

"What!" Miss Pickett cried. "Why, Mr. Coves, I can't raise that amount of money. I was prepared to offer you ten thousand, but your price is out of all reason."

"I'm sorry," said Coves. "Truly I am, and if I didn't need the money so badly, I'd be glad to sell to you. But ten thousand dollars would help me very little. The ten acres to the south of you I've priced at eleven thousand, and I'll gladly sell to you."

"I should think you would," said Miss Pickett indignantly. "I'm sure, Mr. Coves, that your prices are — unrealistic."

Coves said with a trace of vigor, "I'm certain that I can get them, Miss Pickett."

There was a period of bitter silence. The grudging Miss Pickett said,

"Well, if that is your price, Mr. Coves, I have no choice. It's necessary that I provide as much privacy as possible for my school; I'll buy the ten acres from you."

"Thank you," said Coves.

"As soon as you have the deed ready, please let me know and I'll give you a check."

Coves hung up, breathed deeply, turned back to the desk. Waiting was a prosperous-looking gentleman—immaculately groomed, shaved, powdered and pomaded. He had luxuriant black hair, silver at the temples, a handsome face with a hint of a jowl, liquid brown eyes that begged to be believed and trusted. He laid his pigskin gloves on the desk, reached out his white hand.

"My name is Archer, Mr. Coves—Mortimer Archer."

"How do you do?" said Coves.

"I understand, Mr. Coves, that you've placed parts of the island up for sale."

"Why, yes."

"Well, I took the liberty of looking the island over, and it's certainly a beautiful spot. Ideal, really."

"Ah, may I inquire the nature of your interest?"

Mortimer Archer nodded. "Mr. Coves, I'm a retired businessman, and I dabble in photography. I'm looking for a place where I can build a little house and get out into the fresh air with my camera, lead a placid, secluded, relaxed existence."

"There's some wonderful scenery out here," said Coves. He reached under the desk, found the map. "I've sold Blocks One and Two just this morning. But these sections—Three, Four and Five—are still available."

Archer took a pair of horn-rimmed spectacles from his pocket, adjusted them to his nose. "Hm... Ah, yes, I see. What is the price on Three, Mr. Coves?"

Coves coughed. "Well—that's twenty-eight thousand dollars."

Archer blinked. "Did you say twenty-eight thousand?"

"Er, yes...You see, there's twenty-eight acres, and it has this stretch of beach, and all these trees and a great deal of level land—some wonderful building sites."

Archer's mouth dropped at the corners.

"I'm sure the price isn't out of line," said Coves defensively.

Archer hesitated, touching his mustache, gazing absently across the lobby. Almost reluctantly, he reached into his breast pocket, brought forth a wallet. Slowly he counted five twenty-dollar bills down on the counter. "Here's a hundred deposit, Mr. Coves. I'll have a certified check for the balance as soon as I have a report on the title."

"Yes, of course," said Coves. "It's a clear title direct from the state and guaranteed by the state. I'll write you a receipt."

Two hours later the telephone rang. "Bird Island Hotel," said Coves. "Oh hello, Al! What can I do for you?"

"Coves, a relative of mine just pulled in from Alaska — a sort of cousin, I guess. He likes it down here and thought he might buy some property where he can do a little fishing and settle down. I told him about Bird Island, took him around in the launch, and he likes it — especially that little cove at the south end in all the rocks. What's the price on that?"

Coves said, "Why, it's twenty-four thousand dollars, Al. Ah, this cousin of yours, he's — er, all right? I mean — well, you know…"

"Oh, sure," came Al Carper's assurance. "He's the salt of the earth. Just the kind of man you want out there. And he'll pay you right now — in gold dust, if you want it."

"Oh no," said Coves. "I'd rather have a check. I've got so much money out here I don't know what to do with it all."

Carper said, "Just a minute, I'll ask Ike if he wants the cove at twenty-four thousand. There's about twenty acres of land, isn't there?"

"Twenty-four," said Coves.

He heard a mutter of voices. Then Carper returned to the phone.

"He'll take it. We'll get a certified check and bring it out to you today."

Chapter III

Milo Green was a likeable man and Miss Pickett a woman of unalloyed and unswerving virtue. But some personalities are incompatible, and perhaps the two were never fated for friendship.

The initial incident occurred almost at once. Milo was sitting in the lobby of the Val d'Oro Inn in Monterey, where he had registered after finishing his business with Coves. Glancing across the room, he saw a very pretty girl in a brown suit approaching the desk.

The girl was agreeable in every respect. She was slender, flexible. She had citron-tan skin, big solemn dark eyes, brown hair lustrous as Turkish coffee. She wore a brown skirt and jacket with touches of scarlet, and a pair of silly little bronze leather sandals.

She took a key from the clerk, and a bellboy conducted her to the elevator. Milo crossed the lobby to the desk.

"Excuse me," he said to the clerk, "that girl who just registered… who is she?"

The clerk's expression was like a sly nudge with the elbow. "She registered 'Miss Lydia Pickett and party'."

"Who's the party?"

The clerk shrugged. "Hasn't showed yet."

Milo rubbed his chin. "She looks kind of young — for what she's supposed to be."

The clerk shrugged. "Do I look like a hotel clerk?"

Milo saw a gourd-shaped man of forty with a wispy mustache, large glistening teeth. "Why no… More like a — well, civil engineer."

The clerk teetered back and forth on his heels. "That's the story right there. You can't tell much by looks."

Milo, turning away, bumped into a tall, angular woman of indefinite age. She had cold eyes, a nose and chin like the working end of a pipe wrench.

The contact caused the woman to drop her handbag. "Sorry," said Milo. He bent to retrieve the article; she did the same. Their heads collided.

"Umph," said Milo. "Excuse me."

The woman straightened. "I'll get it myself, thank you."

"As you please," said Milo. The woman stooped and seized the bag. The clasp loosened and a tumble of pink lingerie, a long ivory comb, an ivory-backed brush, fell out. A can labeled 'Xtra-Value Epsom Salts' spread its contents.

Milo bent forward. "May I help you?"

"You will oblige me," said the woman, "by getting yourself out of the way."

Milo marched back to his seat at the desk. The woman was shown to her room by a bellboy.

Half an hour later, the girl in brown descended the stairs and pushed through the swinging door into the coffee shop.

Milo gave his jacket a jerk, ran his hands through his hair, and followed briskly.

The girl had settled at a booth and was surveying the menu. Milo slid into the seat opposite her. She glanced up inquiringly.

"I'm Milo Green," said Milo. "One of your neighbors on Bird Island, starting today."

The girl's polite but cool glance became a trifle less guarded. "What part of the island is yours?"

"Section One, the hill at the north end."

"You must have a wonderful view."

"You can see a thousand miles in all directions."

The girl said, "A good place for a television station."

"A better place for the house I'm going to build."

She nodded. "I suppose you'll have big windows?"

"That's right. Windows everywhere." Milo cleared his throat. "Pardon me, I suppose you've heard it a thousand times — but aren't you rather young for what you're doing?"

"I'm twenty. Is that too young?"

"Just right. But I expected something different. Something like the old carp I bumped into out in the lobby. Now she was more my idea of a schoolmistress. Face like a salt-water crocodile, ugly as sin. You'd have busted a stay when she poured her handbag all over the lobby."

"Celia," came a rasping voice by his shoulder, "if you will move to another booth, I'll join you."

Milo blinked and turned his head. Through a fog he heard the girl say, "Auntie, this is Mr. Green. He's just bought part of Bird Island. Mr. Green, my aunt, Miss Pickett."

Milo stumbled to his feet. "Have my seat, Miss Pickett — I've got a phone call to make."

"Goodbye," came Celia's clear voice. "See you again."

"You'll do nothing of the sort," Milo heard Miss Pickett say. "He's an insolent young boor…" Her further remarks were cut off by the swinging doors.

Milo returned to the desk, wiped his sweating palms. He cocked a vindictive eye at the clerk, who was talking to a man in a gray flannel suit. Milo saw the clerk nod in his direction, and the gentleman in gray flannel turned.

"Mr. Green? My name is Archer, Mortimer Archer. I understand we're to be neighbors on Bird Island."

Milo found himself held by the frankest and most lucid of brown eyes, in a face perfectly shaved and talcumed. It was a face of dignity and culture and sympathetic understanding.

"Glad to meet you," said Milo. "Where are you located?"

"Section Three," said Mr. Archer. "And you?"

"Number One… I suppose you're planning to build?"

"Oh yes. Bird Island is the ideal place for my business."

Milo raised his eyebrows. "Business?"

Archer laughed. "Oh, hardly a business. Photography. More a hobby at which I make an odd dollar once in a while."

Milo nodded. "I see."

Archer held out his hand. "Well, good day, Mr. Green. It's been a pleasure. I'm sure we'll be seeing more of each other."

✳

The fog was coming in — long, pale breaths, fleeing the ocean like frightened ghosts. It shrouded the harbor, the wharves, the fishing boats, and formed into banks that penetrated the streets, smelling of wetness and salt, tar and fish.

Celia Marlowe, sauntering down Alvarado Street to Fisherman's Wharf to see what Bird Island looked like, thought the total effect picturesque. As she crossed the street to the pier, she became aware of a diffident shape at her heels.

Without even seeming to glance in his direction, she ascertained that the shape was Milo Green. She adjusted her profile to its best advantage.

Milo drew abreast. "I suppose your aunt is annoyed with me?"

Celia said, without turning her head, "You weren't exactly polite to her."

Milo shoved his hands in his pockets. "I should be more careful... I'll apologize when I see her."

"That would make it worse." After a minute, she said, "I wouldn't worry too much. She'll forget all about you. She's got so much on her mind. You can't imagine how much work is involved in running a school."

Milo looked at her curiously. "Where do you fit in? Are you just visiting?"

"Oh no," said Celia. "I'm to teach."

"Teach! Teach what?"

She shrugged. "Simple things. Elementary music. Badminton. Current events. I'll probably correct papers and — well, just generally help."

Milo took her arm and steered her into a little seafood stand perched over the water on rickety black piles. "Let's have a shrimp cocktail."

They sat at a table covered with a red checked cloth. Milo ordered, leaned back in his chair, scrutinized her with interest. "This is the first time you've been down here?"

"Um-hmm. I'm just out of school."

"And right back into another one."

Celia laughed. "What's wrong with that?"

"Plenty," said Milo soberly. "It's not psychologically healthy to lord it over students all your life. You get pushed behind a barrier, you lose contact; the first thing you know, you're a has-been."

"Somebody's got to do it."

"You're nice the way you are."

"Thanks. But if you're going out to live on a crag, you're not living a normal life either."

"I'm different," said Milo. "I've got a very good reason."

"You don't look too happy about it."

"Well — I more or less bought the place on impulse. Now it's occurred to me that I didn't look far enough ahead."

Celia dipped into the shrimp cocktail. "How do you mean?"

"About two months ago," said Milo, "a bartender gave me a lottery ticket — the Mexican Grand National. It came in. After I paid the taxes I had twenty thousand."

"Why, Milo!" gasped Celia. "How wonderful!"

He shrugged. "I just gave Coves ten thousand. And about an hour ago I signed a contract for a twenty-five thousand dollar house."

"Whew," whistled Celia. "That's a lot of house."

"I'm afraid I acted on impulse. I'll have to pay the bank a hundred a month now. So instead of being twenty thousand to the good, I'm almost twenty thousand in the hole."

"But think of the wonderful house you'll have!"

"If it isn't foreclosed in about a month and a half."

Celia said, "If you work hard, you can pay for it."

Milo sadly shook his head.

"How did you support yourself before?"

"I have a miserable faculty for doggerel which I sell to children's magazines," Milo said.

Celia looked at him with new interest.

"You must be very clever."

"I'm not clever. It's just a knack." He found a pencil, scribbled on a paper napkin. Celia reached out, and read what he had scribbled.

> *Carnations are red,*
> *Delphiniums are blue,*
> *Maple-nut ice cream is delightful*
> *As are you.*

Celia giggled.

"Well," said Milo, "now you see what I mean."

"I think you're very talented," said Celia. "Have you anything with you that's been published?"

Milo rather shamefacedly produced a pair of clippings. "These appeared in last month's *Short Pants Review*."

Celia laid them out on the table and bent her dark head.

"That's cute," she said. She turned to the second, read it, looked up, inspected Milo soberly. "I think they're good. Why, you could go out to Bird Island and very quickly sell enough poetry to pay for your house. Suppose you wrote a volume of poetry that became a children's best seller?"

"That's not realistic," said Milo. "I'd want to write a different kind of stuff."

"What, for instance?"

"Oh..." Milo stared out across the harbor, where the fog had grayed the wharves and put an opalescence on the black water. "Something on a big scale. An epic maybe."

"Well," said Celia doubtfully, "I don't know."

Milo leaned back in his chair. "When do you start work?"

"The spring term commences in a week."

"Is Miss Pickett going to pay you?"

"Of course she's going to pay me."

"Union scale?"

Celia said, "I'm getting very valuable training. So Aunt Lydia says."

Milo snorted and looked out toward Bird Island, now hidden in the fog. "The place seems to be making money hand over fist."

"It's one of the most successful schools in the state," said Celia. "Aunt Lydia's a good manager. Her fees are high, and she's very strict." There was a pause. Celia moved restlessly. "I'd better be getting back."

They walked out on the wharf, stood looking across the harbor. The water was black below and the fog was dank in their faces.

"My, but it's spooky," said Celia. "I'll bet there are ghosts in Monterey."

"I should think so," said Milo. "It's the oldest town in California." He looked down at her. "Do you know there's supposed to be treasure out on Bird Island?"

"No… Is there?"

"That's right. The contractor was telling me. Nobody knows where it is, how much it is, anything about it. Just that Bird Island used to be owned by a gang of bootleggers, and that when they were put in jail, they left a lot of money on Bird Island."

Celia said with a grin, "If you find the treasure, you can pay off your bank."

Milo snapped his fingers. "I've got a good idea. Let's look for the treasure tomorrow."

"How do we get there? Swim?"

"I have a boat. It's out there in the harbor now. You can't see it in the fog."

"Well… all right. But we'll have to keep it quiet from Aunt Lydia."

They returned to the Val d'Oro. Coves stood in the lobby reading a letter. He raised his hand affably. "Ah, Mr. Green."

"Hello, Mr. Coves." Milo introduced Celia. "How's business?"

"I've sold everything," said Coves.

"My," said Milo, "that's quick work."

"It certainly was," said Coves. "I'm starting alterations on the hotel tomorrow."

"And who are the other buyers?"

"Well, let's see… There's you, of course, and Mr. Archer." Coves tapped the names off his plump fingers. "Then Mr. — let's see, Al Carper's cousin — Mr. O'Rourke. And Mr. Ottenbright, a San Francisco lawyer. And Miss Pickett took the small section next to her school." He looked at his watch. "Perhaps you'll be my guests at dinner. I think practically all — if not all — of the new Bird Islanders will be there. It'll be a nice occasion to get acquainted."

"Thanks," said Milo. "I'd be delighted."

Celia hesitated. "My aunt…"

"Oh yes, she's been invited."

"Then I'll be glad to come."

"In about an hour then. I've reserved a big table in the alcove to the rear of the restaurant."

CHAPTER IV

THE DINNER GUESTS were a multifarious lot, with qualities ranging from Mortimer Archer's finished elegance to the more elemental vigor of Ike O'Rourke, who wore a bushy yellow beard over his checkered mackinaw and who spoke knowingly of tundras and igloos and dog sleds.

Miss Pickett, in a severe suit of black serge, was the last to appear. Coves introduced her to her new neighbors, starting with a portly gentleman with dewlaps and a balding pate, and his equally portly spouse.

"Miss Pickett, Mr. and Mrs. Ottenbright."

Then: "Miss Pickett, Mr. Green."

"I have already met Mr. Green." Miss Pickett's voice rang with an iron vibration.

Coves brought forward Ike O'Rourke. "Miss Pickett, may I present Mr. O'Rourke?"

"Pleased to meetcha," said Ike O'Rourke.

Miss Pickett turned a look of accusation at Coves, whose forehead shone with little beads of sweat. Now Coves brought forward Mortimer Archer.

"Miss Pickett, Mr. Archer."

Mr. Archer took her hand, smiling gently. "Miss Pickett."

A waiter signaled to Coves. "Dinner is served," said Coves.

Conversation during the meal was dominated jointly by Miss Pickett and Mr. Ottenbright. In the fruity baritone which had hypnotized a hundred juries, Mr. Ottenbright described a recent case, fixing Milo with humid blue eyes. Miss Pickett, at the other end of the table, engaged Mr. Archer with her theories of academic discipline.

"It was a sorry spectacle," said Mr. Ottenbright, tapping Milo's wrist. "This popinjay Clevinger wouldn't rest — the most witless excuse for an attorney I've ever seen. For two entire hours he argued and made an ass of himself, until the judge —"

"— chewing gum I have never tolerated," Miss Pickett impressed upon Mr. Archer. "It is my strict rule that whenever an instructor discovers a student engaging in the practice, he must direct her to paste the substance to her forehead and wear it till the end of the period —"

"— I cited Snyder versus Crum Salvage. But Clevinger, in the same obstinate rut, contended the inapposition of —"

"— I allow one dollar and twenty-five cents spending money per week. More than ample for —"

Ike O'Rourke's belch was like the bark of a seal. "This is good grub, Mr. Coves," he said.

Miss Pickett frowned. Mr. Ottenbright wiped his mouth with a flourish.

"Well," said Ike, "I been over to the island and I like it. Nice breeze blows in off the ocean, ideal climate for whales. I'm anxious to get my plant started."

"Whales?" Miss Pickett raised her eyebrows. "What 'plant' is this, Mr. O'Rourke?"

"Renderin' plant. I decided that besides herdin' and raisin' whales, I'd do my own slaughterin' and renderin'."

Coves' face became pale. "Surely —" he started, but Miss Pickett's tones cut through.

"Mr. O'Rourke, do you realize that such a course would be grossly unfair to those of us who depend upon public patronage for our living?"

Ike's face set into an expression of mulish obstinacy. "Don't see why."

Mr. Ottenbright cleared his throat. "I fear, Mr. O'Rourke, that your project is not practical. Certain laws regulate such enterprises, and I believe that anyone situated in such a way that the wind blew from you to him could obtain a cease-and-desist injunction with a minimum of effort."

"The wind don't blow all the time."

"Just the idea," sniffed Miss Pickett, "would keep well-bred girls away from my academy."

"Well, if you're being so dang fussy," said Ike, "I guess I'll just corral me a herd and sell them to the plant."

Milo said in an awed tone, "How do you go about catching a herd of whales, Mr. O'Rourke?"

Ike winked. "It's an old Eskimo trick, lad. They know lots of things up north they ain't expected to know. They live good and they eat good. Why? Because they knows fish, they knows all about fish...I learned a lot, but I'll never get the science of it like some of them old witch doctors."

"But where will you keep these whales after you've caught them?"

"I got a nice cove right there on my property. I'll sink some piles, string some cable across and there'll be my pen. Then I'll go out, lure me in ten or twelve whale, and all I got to do is wait, and maybe they'll breed some young 'uns."

"Suppose they won't cooperate?" suggested Celia mischievously.

"Hah!" said Ike. "Don't worry none about that, girl. I got what it takes to make 'em cooperate."

"Er, Mr. O'Rourke," said Mr. Archer.

"Yes sir?"

"Won't the whales starve? How will you feed them? I should imagine that the cove would soon be exhausted of fish."

"Whales don't eat fish. They eats little floating stuff, and it don't matter whether they swims for it or the tide brings it to 'em."

Miss Pickett snorted in disgust. "Whales! The very idea!"

Coves said feebly, "I had no idea...I thought you were interested in fishing, Mr. O'Rourke."

"Well, whales is fish," snapped Ike. He darted a bitter glance at Miss Pickett. "Mind you, I won't allow any of your pesky gals a-comin' over to ask silly questions, like how do I tell a mama from a papa, or why don't whales eat seaweed!"

"Your instructions are unnecessary," snapped Miss Pickett. "My students will be forbidden to entertain even the idea."

"Come, come," chided Mr. Ottenbright. "Ladies and gentlemen! I'm sure no one intends to be uncooperative in any way."

"Of course not," said Mr. Archer.

Coffee and dessert were served.

"Have you decided on whether you'll live out on the island, Mr. Archer?" inquired Miss Pickett.

"It has occurred to me, Miss Pickett, that Bird Island, with its scenic beauties, is a subject that demands the recording eye of a camera. Perhaps I'll establish a small studio and compile a portfolio of studies. During this time I'll live out on the island."

Miss Pickett's eye flicked past Milo as if he had been the bus boy. "And Mr. Ottenbright?"

"Oh — our place will be just a week-end home, where we can come and rest once in a while."

Miss Pickett nodded, rested her eyes briefly on Ike O'Rourke, then turned a scathing glance on Coves.

Coves avoided the gaze.

After dinner Celia spoke to Milo in the lobby. "I can't go with you tomorrow."

"Why not?"

"Aunt Lydia is speaking at the Carmel Community Center tomorrow afternoon, and she wants me to drive her."

"Why doesn't she drive herself?"

"You'll have to ask her."

Milo ran his fingers through his hair. "We could go in the morning and be back by noon."

She looked at him with a half-smile, and Milo wanted to lean forward and kiss her.

"Are we actually going to look for treasure?"

"Why not?"

"But we don't have any map, and we can't dig up the whole beach."

"I can see you've a very practical mind."

"Somebody's got to use their head. And you're a poet." Celia threw a glance over her shoulder. "Here comes Aunt Lydia. I don't think she wants me to associate with you."

"Celia!" came a sharp voice.

"See you tomorrow morning," said Milo.

Celia sat up with a jerk, brown curls tousled around her face. From the angular hulk of Miss Pickett came a groan. "What is it?" she asked hollowly.

Celia leapt to the phone. "Hello?" she said in a guarded whisper.

"Time to get up," said Milo. "I'll be waiting in the lobby."

"Who in the world is calling at this time of night?" rasped Miss Pickett.

"Wrong number," said Celia.

Miss Pickett groaned once more, lapsed to the pillow.

Celia went to her bed and sat shivering on the edge. What time was it? She peered through the window. Low at the horizon a vague glimmer of dawn had appeared.

"That fool," muttered Celia. "That fool…" Cautiously she gathered up her clothes and crept into the bathroom. She doused her face with cold water, brushed her teeth, combed her hair, dressed in blue jeans, a white blouse, a green pull-over. Quietly she left the bathroom.

"Celia," said a very wide-awake voice, "just what are you doing?"

Celia put her hand on the doorknob. "Taking a walk, Auntie. You go back to sleep." She passed out the door.

Celia fled to the lobby, careless of the dressing-down she knew she would face later in the day. Milo was standing by the desk, talking with the night clerk.

"Milo, you devil," said Celia. "Let's go before my aunt comes chasing down the stairs after me."

They raced out the big glass doors into the gray morning, turned down the street toward the harbor. The fog had vanished. The only sound was the *slip-slap* of waves against the sea wall and the scuff of their footsteps.

As they hurried along, the pallid sky deepened to saffron and small chalky streaks of cloud took on the color of geranium petals. They descended the steps to the landing — "Oh hell," said Milo, and his voice rang across the air.

"What's the trouble?"

"Look," said Milo. "That's my boat out there at the mooring."

"How do we get out there?"

Milo compressed his lips thoughtfully. "We'll borrow one of these dinghies."

Celia looked at him sidelong. "No one has given us permission to use his boat."

"Come on!" He jumped down to the water's edge, waved at her.

"Here's just the right boat for us." He hauled a round-bottomed little dinghy into the landing.

"I'm not coming," said Celia, looking down at him. "I don't want to be arrested."

Milo shrugged, bent over, untied the painter from the bow. He felt the boat lurch and when he looked up, Celia was settling herself in the stern.

Milo cast off. He thought, If I hand her one of these paddles, from sheer contrariness she'll refuse to touch it. Aloud he said, "You just sit still and enjoy the ride. I don't want you to get your hands dirty."

Celia determinedly took up a paddle. "Nothing in the world could stop me from paddling."

Milo said nothing. Now the only sounds were the ripple of the bow, the *drip-drip-drip* from their paddles.

They drew alongside Milo's sloop, and Milo steadied the dinghy while Celia jumped aboard; then he followed. Ship the rudder, hoist the sail, drop the mooring. The sail pulled, the boat swung easily. They towed the dinghy back to the landing, then came about, set sail for Bird Island.

They were quiet a while, with the water surging and bubbling at the bow and the wake pulling up astern. Celia laughed in sheer exhilaration.

"This is wonderful, Milo... I'm glad you did get me up in the middle of the night. Even if I was mad at the time. And what if we actually do find the treasure!"

Milo nodded. "It's probably gold. Doubloons, *louis d'or*, crowns, pieces of eight. Treasure usually is gold."

Celia said, "Bootleggers wouldn't bury pieces of eight... I'd prefer jewels, anyway."

Bird Island drew nearer.

The boat slid alongside Miss Pickett's dock. Milo let the halyard go and the sails rattled down the mast. Celia jumped to the dock and Milo tossed her a line which she made fast.

"We must be alone on the island," said Milo, joining her on the dock. "The academy and the hotel are both closed down and nobody's around, except for maybe a caretaker or two."

"So much the better," said Celia. "I hate crowds…Where do we look first?"

"Let's go up to where I'm building my house," said Milo. "We'll get our bearings from there."

They set out up the hill and the dawn became sunrise, and the sun came up into the world bit by bit, the same way it had sunk the night before, and the golden light shone on their backs as they scrambled up the rocks.

"Here we are," panted Milo. "Look at the Pacific out there…"

"It's beautiful," gasped Celia, sitting on a stone and pushing her dark curls back. "Is this where you're going to build?"

"Right here on this very spot."

Celia looked down the slope of the hill, across the bay to the mainland. "Won't it be expensive bringing all the material up here?"

"We've got that angle licked," said Milo. "The contractor will prefabricate everything possible at his yard and fly it out."

She turned her head to look at him. "Fly it out?"

"Helicopter," said Milo. "Freight-carrying helicopter. We'll bring the whole house out in a day. Of course I'm planning to use a lot of this native rock —" He stopped short.

"What's the matter?" asked Celia.

"Look," said Milo. "Down there on Coves' beach."

A man was walking slowly along the long white strand, casting a gaunt shadow in the low glare of the sunlight. His eyes were on the sand at the tidemark; he appeared to be searching for something. He stooped, picked up an object which glittered briefly, thrust it into a pouch he carried on his shoulder.

"It's Mr. Archer," whispered Celia. "What on earth is he doing?"

"I don't know," said Milo.

"Let's go down and find out."

They ran down the hill to the beach, jumped out on the crisp sand. Something glittered at Celia's feet. She picked it up. It was a small bottle, tightly capped. Inside was a bit of paper with the number "82" plainly visible.

Mr. Archer had seen them, and was coming across the sand, a curious expression on his face.

"Good morning," said Milo. "What brings you out this time of day?"

"Early-morning constitutional, Mr. Green…Good morning, Miss Marlowe."

"What are you looking for?" Celia asked. "These glass bottles?" She displayed the one she had picked up.

Archer's face flickered. His mustache twitched, his cheek muscles quivered. "Well, I haven't been exactly looking for them," he said. "I've been picking up odds and ends — among them one or two of those bottles. I guess I'm a magpie at heart."

"Almost anything looks interesting on a beach," said Milo. "Coves told me he gets the flotsam and jetsam of half the Pacific on his beach."

Celia examined the bottle. "I wonder what the number means."

Archer's eyes fixed on the bottle. He put out his hand, but Celia appeared not to notice it. He turned away.

"Milo," said Celia, "let's look for some more." She gazed along the sand.

Archer said, "I noticed something very interesting up the beach. A tremendous sea anemone. Purple and red, magnificent! Like a tiger lily. It's worth looking at. I wish I had brought my camera."

"They're dangerous," said Celia. "They'll sting you."

Archer watched the slim figure in blue jeans wandering up the beach. She bent, picked up another bottle, put it in her pocket. Mr. Archer breathed deeply.

"Might as well join the fun," he said and started up the beach after her.

Milo squinted after him thoughtfully. "Oh, Mr. Archer!"

Archer paused, turned his head. "What?"

"Have you seen anyone else on the island this morning?"

Archer turned all the way around. "What's that?"

"We thought we saw someone up on top of the hill," said Milo soberly. "Whoever it was didn't want anyone to see him."

Archer put his hand up to his face and glanced up the hillside. The shadows were dark under the wind-anguished cypress. Great rocks loomed and lowered.

"I haven't seen anyone," he said.

"It might have been a shadow, or a sheep," said Milo.

Archer nodded with his old assurance. "I rather doubt if anyone else is abroad so early. Only a few of us enjoy these morning hours." He glanced toward Celia, who was bending again — and again. She was far up the beach.

"I think I'll be getting back," said Mr. Archer. "Good morning, Mr. Green."

"See you later."

Milo watched the spare figure striding toward Coves' dock, then turned and jogged down the beach toward Celia.

"Look, Milo," she said. "Six bottles. All numbered. Fourteen — eighty-seven — sixty-three — twenty-nine — twenty-two — and eighty-two."

"They evidently came in on the tide."

"But who'd put numbers in bottles in the first place?"

"I can't imagine."

The sun shone fair and the ocean glittered. Celia, looking out to sea, said, "Milo?"

"What?"

"Let's not look for treasure today. Let's go back to your boat and sail out, way out into the ocean. It looks so peaceful and wide and sunny out there."

"Suits me," said Milo.

Surveyors squinted through transits, shouted, waved their arms. Chain-men plodded up and down hill, thumped stakes into the damp black earth. Bulldozers rooted into the crackling gorse, and mounds of ocher clay remained when they had gone. Carpenters strung lines; laborers dug trenches. Foundations were poured, joists placed, subfloors nailed, walls raised, sheathing laid on. Then rafters and roofs, and new houses existed on Bird Island.

Milo's house was low, flat-roofed, with walls of redwood and native stone, and unless one looked closely, it seemed a part of the crag, so low was its outline. Archer's house was a plain white cottage, while the Ottenbrights had erected a pretentious ultra-contemporary beach house, with a wide flagged patio, big brick boxes planted with azaleas and begonias.

The old Bird Island Hotel was lost in the new construction. Wings sprouted off at either side and the old steep-gabled roof now spread out in a modern silhouette. The creaking veranda had given way to a broad terrace running the length of the hotel, and a lavish bar opened off the lobby. For the terrace, Coves had bought two dozen wrought-iron and glass tables with chairs to match and two-dozen sun umbrellas in carnival colors. A tennis court and swimming pool occupied the meadow behind the hotel, and three new broad-beamed sailboats were tied to the dock for the convenience of nautically minded guests.

Ike O'Rourke had built himself a two-room cabin of unfinished pine, with a tar-paper roof. An adjoining lath and chicken-wire pen housed his three dogs. Across the entrance to the cove a pile driver on a barge had pounded a line of piles, lashed and meshed with heavy wire rope. Pontoons supported a gate which could be opened from the twenty-foot launch Ike had purchased in Monterey.

The new construction, of course, had not been completed in a day, a week, a month. Events had intervened. Madeline Cheabrough had registered at Miss Pickett's Academy. Fougasse came to occupy the post of *chef de cuisine* at Bird Island Hotel. And even Rexie the cat had his troubles.

CHAPTER V

THE ROSTER OF THE ACADEMY was at all times crowded, and only as a favor to Mrs. Cheabrough, herself a former student, did Miss Pickett consent to enroll Madeline for the spring term. The three stood on the sea wall looking out across the bay to Bird Island. Miss Pickett wore her customary black serge suit, with black flat-heeled shoes. Mrs. Cheabrough, a buxom woman with a stylish bust, was securely wrapped in the skins of dead animals. Madeline — a slim girl of seventeen, deceptively quiet, with long yellow hair, a pointed face with an expression designed to drive young men to drink — wore a gray flannel skirt and a pale blue cashmere cardigan.

Miss Pickett had given Mrs. Cheabrough her field glasses for a look at Bird Island. "And those other buildings — what are they?" inquired Mrs. Cheabrough.

Miss Pickett sniffed. "The construction on the crag will be the residence of a Mr. Green. The smaller house at the far left is the studio of Mr. Archer, really a gentleman. Behind the hill the Ottenbrights are —"

"Oh, Mother!" exclaimed Madeline. "Look at the cute boys!"

Mrs. Cheabrough complaisantly inspected a passing convertible with a crimson "Stanford" pasted to the windshield. Madeline turned to Miss Pickett. "I'm sure we'll have ever so many parties and dances at the academy, won't we, Miss Pickett?"

"Of course, darling," said Mrs. Cheabrough, whose memory of her years at Miss Pickett's had been mellowed by the passage of time. "Miss Pickett understands that young folk like good times."

Miss Pickett's mouth looked like a reef knot. "Primarily, of course, the academy emphasizes its scholastic and cultural program — but I expect —" the words dragged themselves forth reluctantly "— a few quiet affairs will be arranged."

"Nothing elaborate of course," agreed Mrs. Cheabrough. "One reason I withdrew Madeline from the Sark Institute was their Midsummer Festival. Eight days, think of it! No, I fancy you plan nothing more than a weekly cotillion, perhaps a tennis party, a picnic, two or three formal dances a term. Am I right?"

"Well, of course I expect the girls to enjoy themselves…"

Mrs. Cheabrough did not appear to be listening. "I'm sure, Miss Pickett, you'll think I'm a foolish old woman, and I know you want to be liberal — but I like Madeline to be in nights by twelve."

"Oh, Mother," said Madeline disgustedly, "what's the difference? Miss Pickett is up to date on things like that."

Mrs. Cheabrough shrugged. "Well, Miss Pickett knows best. But I'm sure she'll insist on a curfew, at least during the week."

Miss Pickett found her voice. "Mrs. Cheabrough, you labor under the delusion that —"

"Mother, look!" breathed Madeline. "Those boys are flirting with me! See them looking over here and smiling?"

Mrs. Cheabrough gave the situation a swift glance. "No darling, I'm afraid not. It's Miss Pickett at whom they're smiling. I'm afraid her slip is showing."

"Oh," said Madeline. Miss Pickett, after a shocked inspection over her shoulder, swept off toward the hotel.

The catalogue of courses described Miss Celia Marlowe, A.B., as instructor for History of Music, Elements of Harmony, A Survey of Oriental Literature, Tennis: Beginners and Advanced. In addition to these formal duties, Celia found herself expected to correct and grade themes, essays, term papers for the English department, and in her spare moments, to manage Miss Pickett's correspondence.

Infused by enthusiasm, Celia enjoyed the first few weeks — though authority over girls at most four years her junior was strange and uncomfortable. Then the more routine of her duties began to pall. The themes read like the essays and the essays like the themes. Miss Pickett's correspondence lost its fascination.

Theoretically she was free Saturday afternoons and Sundays, but there seemed to be a succession of week-end emergencies which demanded her attention.

Sunday. A bright sunny morning. Celia, just out of bed, was brushing her hair. She counted the last five strokes aloud, put down the brush. "Hello," she said to the mirror. "I think you're rather pretty, more than not..." She experimented, tightening her cheek muscles, pursing her lips. She jumped up from the dressing table, swirled her dressing gown close around her hips, walked away, watching over her shoulder. Everything was satisfactory. She threw off her robe, hopped out of her pajamas into dark green pedal-pushers, a loose dark green blouse.

An assertive rapping at her door. "Celia!" Miss Pickett was in her most executive mood.

"Yes?"

"I'm going across to Monterey to sign for some books, and I want you to type up the letters I dictated yesterday."

"But Aunt Lydia —"

"They're very important; they should have been out Friday."

"Okay," growled Celia.

Miss Pickett departed and Celia trotted downstairs to the dining room, ate breakfast, loitered over coffee. She sighed. Miss Pickett had undoubtedly dictated enough letters to keep her busy all day. Celia played morosely with the silverware. Typing was a dull business, and it was a wonderful day outside, with a light breeze from the direction of Honolulu.

She dragged herself to the office. This was divided into two sections: Miss Pickett's private office and an outer office. Miss Pickett's private office was locked, together with the dictation.

Celia shrugged. Too bad, Aunt Lydia. The keys were in Miss Pickett's bureau, but it wouldn't be nice to go through all her drawers. With Miss Pickett out of the way, there were things to do, people to see. She ran down the stairs, out the door — quickly.

She was out in the open air, and free. She strode briskly across the meadow, climbed through an open woods of cypress, and breasted to the crest of the sway-backed ridge.

In front of her lay the hotel and the long white beach, behind her the academy. To the right and up was Milo's house of redwood, glass and gray rock.

She came to Milo's house, approached a door of russet planks almost as thick and heavy as railroad ties. After a moment of tingling hesitation, she pressed the bell button.

The door presently opened. Milo looked out. "Oh, hello…Come on in."

Celia sidled through the door into a room floored with red tile, and furnished with a massive refectory table and six leather-and-oak chairs. The far end of the room was dim. Stepping forward, Celia found herself overlooking a large living room with wide windows opening on the blue, white and green expanse.

"How lovely!" said Celia fervently. "And what lovely banisters! Or —" doubtfully "— is it a balustrade?"

"Balustrade," said Milo. "A baluster is a single support of a balustrade, the word 'banister' being a corruption of 'baluster'."

"You slide down banisters."

"True," said Milo. "Or rather, you slide down the balustrade of a staircase."

"I'll take the banisters, and I bet I get down first."

Milo ignored the challenge.

Celia's mood changed. "Oh Milo, what an absolutely wonderful house!"

Milo's air of vague dissatisfaction lifted. "You like it?"

"It's marvelous!"

Milo shrugged. "It would have been better if I'd had a sensible architect. Dray fought me at every turn. Come on, I'll show you around."

Celia followed him past the long refectory table, which was waxed till it glistened like a pool of oil. To the right a waist-high counter separated them from a kitchen with walls painted dark green. The range, sink, cabinets were enameled terra cotta; windows opposite opened out to the bay.

"I wanted a livelier tone for all that stuff," grumbled Milo. "Vermilion, or yellow. Dray insisted on that rusty stuff."

"It's lovely, Milo! It's warm and restful. I think Mr. Dray has very good taste."

Milo sniffed. They descended to the living room.

"I had to bargain with Dray," said Milo. "He had his way upstairs, vice versa downstairs…This is the living room. Dray and I agreed on the furniture." These were low and massive pieces — dark wood upholstered with a tough natural colored cloth.

Celia inspected the room with interest. The wall across from her was bare plaster, but evident were the first steps of a fresco. A rectangle had been lined out, a design blocked out on a grid. Milo noticed her interest.

"It'll be plants and flowers in bastard-Rousseau," he told her gloomily. "I wanted a plaque in the Persian style. Dray saw my sketches and made me promise to put in nothing but those damn vegetables."

"I'm sure it will turn out nicely, Milo," Celia soothed him. "I think the house is perfect."

Milo looked away. "Well I'm glad. Because eventually — perhaps — you'll be living here." He became absorbed in the view.

"What?"

"It's not impossible that we might — be married," said Milo, intent on the flight of a distant sea gull.

"Milo!" cried Celia, in a queer voice. "Are you proposing to me?"

"Proposals should be unnecessary," said Milo.

"How is a girl supposed to know then?" Her voice was hushed, rich, warm. "When she sees someone she likes, I suppose she says, 'Since proposals are such obsolete blunders, if you'd like to get married, let's not waste any time'?"

"It should be a mutual understanding. Rapport. A telepathic intimation of singularity."

"People have to be in love before they marry," said Celia.

"See those window boxes? That's where I'm going to plant geraniums," said Milo vaguely.

"Milo!" snapped Celia.

"What?"

"Oh…nothing. Show me your house."

He led her to a flight of stairs of lustrous maroon tile, each set with a sign of the Zodiac in red, blue, green and yellow glazes.

"Here Dray's area of authority ends," Milo told Celia at the landing. "Everything below is more or less to my personal plan."

"What are those funny little masks, Milo? They're — scary."

"Mahmoud Singh designed them —"

"Who's Mahmoud Singh?"

"He's a very good friend of mine — a Hindu. I've invited him to visit me as soon as he can get away. It was his idea to hang those masks along the staircase. They're gods, Hindu gods. The fat one with the elephant head is Ganesa; then comes Vishnu, and Siva, and Brahma with the three heads, and Kali, the demon of vengeance. Tough, isn't she?" Milo paused before the leering visage. "Then — the one playing the fiddle is Krishna — and here we are at the bottom. Ahead of us is the study."

They entered a room paneled with dark wood, furnished with a deep leather lounge, a desk, a chair, shelves of books. A carpet of dark green covered the floor; there was a fireplace with bronze andirons. It was a room designed for long, dark midnights by the light of glowing coals.

Celia looked around without enthusiasm. "I'd put up some bright draperies and paint all that woodwork white. It would be so much more cheerful."

"Sit down," said Milo. "I'll mix us drinks at the bar."

"I want to see the bar," said Celia.

"First, you sit still," said Milo mysteriously. "Then you see the bar."

So Celia sat on the big leather lounge and waited. Milo vanished into an alcove. Celia caught a glimpse of polished wood, the flash of bottles. She twisted, scanned the books behind the couch. *The Works of Shakespeare*, the *Pigeon-Breeders' Gazette* (1932-1936), bound in brown buckram, Plato's *Republic*, *The Critique of Pure Reason*, a book called *Atlantis, the Antediluvian World* by Ignatius Donnelly.

A gentle *click-click-click* caught her ear.

Twisting her head, she found a toy electric locomotive pulling a flatcar down a track behind the couch. Two highballs rode the flatcar.

The train stopped directly behind her back.

Milo joined her. "It runs behind the couch, then back to the bar again."

"Milo," said Celia gravely, "how much did all this cost?"

Milo sat back and tasted his highball. "Complete with liquor, canned goods, typewriter, rugs, a few other items, like floor wax, fly swatters, shovels — by the way, did you see the road I'm building? I dig two hours every morning before breakfast."

"Milo."

"Well — twenty-seven thousand, eight hundred and sixty-five dollars. Some odd cents."

Celia sighed.

Milo raised his eyebrows. "I work six hours a day, slave over the typewriter till the sweat runs off me —"

Celia melted. "Oh Milo, I know you're working. But have you accomplished anything?"

Milo gulped at his drink. "That's a good highball, if I did mix it myself."

"Milo," said Celia, "you were telling me about what you were writing."

"Oh, yes. Well, it's a ballad — about a man who wanted to buy himself a new hat."

"Tell me about it. What's the plot?"

"Just a regular ballad plot. Joy, sorrow, tears and mirth."

"Such as?"

"Well, it's divided into three parts, with a Prologue and an Envoi. The Prologue runs like this: A man decided to buy a hat. He went to the store, but nothing suited him. The clerk showed him everything in the place — fedoras, homburgs, top hats, derbies; tarbooshes, cloth caps, busbies, billycocks, shakos, fezzes, Tyroleans and turbans; sombreros, coonskins, and Panamas. Nothing suited him. The sombreros were too wide, the homburgs too narrow. The derbies too sedate; the toppers too pretentious, the turbans too eccentric. Finally he strolled to another counter, looked at some handkerchiefs, bought a tie clasp, and walked out. The salesman was furious. Presently another customer approached, an innocent young man from the country, fresh-faced, inclined to corpulence. The salesman says, 'Yes, sir-r-r-r?' The young man says, 'I've been invited to dinner by my boss, who is also, I hope, my future father-in-law. It's quite a formal affair, and I require a suitable piece of headgear. What would you suggest?'

"The salesman brings out an immense Gainsborough hat of blue velvet, with a purple ribbon and a long blue plume. 'Just the thing, sir,' he says.

" 'You don't think it's extreme?' inquires the young man.

" 'The latest mode, sir,' replies the vindictive salesman.

"The young man buys it and wears it proudly to the formal dinner, where of course he draws all eyes. His boss bawls him out, the girl he loves sneers at him, and his life is ruined. And that," Milo concluded, "finishes the Prologue." He glanced at Celia. "Do you like it?"

Celia nodded. "That's very nice, Milo. What's the rest of it?"

Milo settled back. "Well—Harvey Rotherhyde changes. The setback molds his character. He becomes dour and crafty, revengeful. He returns to his chicken ranch and plots. This is in Stanza One. In Stanza Two his plans mature. He loads the back of his truck with brooding hens, and in the dead of night drives to the city. He parks at the back entrance to the store, which he pries open. Then:

> With his cargo of hens,
> Direct from their pens,
> He steals through the store to Furnishings, Men's.

"Now he upturns all the hats on the shelves, and in each he places a hen and a setting of eggs. The hens settle themselves, cluck once or twice, and Rotherhyde steals away. That's Stanza Two.

"Next begins Stanza Three. A watchman sees him leaving the store and raises an outcry. A mounted policeman takes up the chase.

"Rotherhyde is clever and resourceful, dodges into dark alleys, hides in garbage cans, generally keeps the policeman guessing. But always the thunder of hoofs draws closer and closer. At last he runs to a large hotel, pushes in through the revolving door and registers under the name of Claude Jenkins. The policeman, his horse all lathered and flaring at the nostril, tears around until at last he discovers where Rotherhyde has fled. But:

> Riding through the revolving door
> Delayed the policeman even more.

"Little trick to the meter there," Milo said. "Can't seem to straighten it out. But anyway, the policeman jumps out of the saddle, asks the clerk, 'Did a Harvey Rotherhyde come in here?'

"The clerk says, 'No one by that name registered, sir.'

"The policeman is puzzled and uncertain, but at last he leaves, and Harvey Rotherhyde falls in love with the chambermaid, who, so it turns out, is his original girl friend's younger sister, learning the hotel game from the ground up. And that's the end." He settled back on the couch and drained his glass.

Celia nibbled at her ice. "It's a wonderful plot...But is there any market for that kind of thing? Where will you sell it?"

"Darned if I know."

Celia stirred. "Let's go back to the living room. I love to look out those windows."

"I've got a pair of binoculars," said Milo.

They stood together looking out over the ocean. Celia had the binoculars to her eyes. She put them down and turned to speak to Milo. He was looking at her with an expression that stopped the words at her lips.

The telephone rang. It was Miss Pickett. "Mr. Green," she asked in a voice which rattled the diaphragm, "is my niece in your house? If so, I would like to speak to her."

"Just a minute, I'll look." He turned to Celia. "Your aunt wants to know if you're here. Shall I say you're not here?"

"No, I'm caught. Let me talk to her. Hello, Auntie."

Milo could hear the rasp of the voice, see the expressions passing across Celia's face.

Celia hung up at last. "Well, that's that. She says I'm to leave your house at once, and never come back without a suitable chaperone. She says the reputation of the school would suffer if anyone knew about our goings-on."

"Let's get married, then. And you can quit."

She looked out over the horizon.

Milo clenched his jaw. "I know. I'm no good..."

"It's not that, Milo. It's the circumstances. Things are so — unromantic. I want to know that I'm — well, *wanted* before I get married. Not just an escape from an unpleasant situation."

Milo said, "I do want you, Celia."

"You've never said so before, Milo."

She turned toward the door, moving slowly. He sprang after her.

"Oh, Milo…"

At last they separated.

CHAPTER VI

MILO AND CELIA WALKED slowly down Coves' beach. To their right, the surf came lolloping up in gorgeous white foam, only to hasten back in hissing layers. Jellyfish sparkled in the wet. Kelp lay strung out like forlorn old clothes.

At the end of the beach they climbed over a shoulder of rock, then up a slope thatched with heather and blooming with blue lupines. They passed through a huddle of cypress, climbed a bluff, and were looking down on Ike O'Rourke's cove.

Smoke poured from his chimney, a boat bumped at his pier. Ike himself left the cabin, stretched his arms to the sunlight, thrust his yellow beard up so that the wind could tickle his neck. He turned back, entered the cabin, emerged with a bucket and marched toward his launch. He started the engine, pushed off, chuffed to the center of the cove, and the *putt-putt-putt* rose sharp and clear to the ears of Milo and Celia.

The engine stopped and Ike threw out the anchor. Celia and Milo started down the hillside, jumping from rock to rock; in a few minutes they were standing on a small bluff overlooking the cove. To right and left, miniature headlands jutted out to sea, connected by a double row of piles, webbed and lashed and braced with great throws of steel cable.

"Mr. O'Rourke!" called Celia.

"Ike!" yelled Milo.

Ike O'Rourke jerked about in his boat; they found two black holes gaping at them—the muzzle of a double-barreled ten-gauge shotgun. Ike relaxed, replaced the gun along the thwart. He waved an arm, heaved in his anchor and gave the motor a twist.

Presently, with Celia and Milo beside him, he was steering back to the center of the cove.

"You gotta excuse my hurry with the scatter-gun," said Ike. "Fact is, I'm just a *leetle* inclined to be suspicious."

"Suspicious? What of?" asked Milo.

"Suppose you tell me." His yellow beard thrust aggressively forward. "I'd like to know. I see something sneakin' around, an' I know there ain't no bear on this here little island. When I go to look, nothing's there. Well," he shrugged, "I don't like to turn my dogs loose, or they'd just natcherly take over the island. So I keep my gun ready."

"What are you doing out here in your boat, Mr. O'Rourke?" Celia asked.

"Just catching me a batch of fish. Something to throw in the pot."

"Where's your line? Don't you need a line and a hook?"

"Not the way we do it up north," said Ike. He produced a large tin horn from under the seat, inserted the mouthpiece through his whiskers and blew a hoarse blast at the surface of the water. "That calls 'em. Fish is curious, same as men. They want to know what's comin' off. Then I got this net here, and I pick out the critter I like the look of." He leaned over the gunwale, net ready.

"Hm," said Ike, "they're kinda lazy today. Well, I'll give 'em another blast." He did so. *Fwaaaap.*

Swash! Splash! A silver shape left the water, gleamed instantly in the sunlight, plunged below.

"There's a nice bass," said Ike. "Well, let's see what else is around." *Swash!*

"There's a salmon." He leaned over, swept at the water with his net, swung the wriggling shape into the boat. He winked wisely. "There's supper for tonight and lunch tomorrow."

"That's wonderful," marveled Milo. "How did you learn that trick?"

"From the Eskimos. I tell you, they *knows* fish."

"I've never seen anything like it!" said Celia.

Ike shrugged. "I could train 'em if I wanted to. Up north I've seen good salmon that'll follow a man like a dog, yap and grunt when they see him. If they had legs, they'd come up on the bank. They're real pets, if you take a little trouble with 'em." He started up the engine, swung the wheel, ran alongside the ramshackle dock, tied up.

"Aren't you lonely here, all by yourself?" asked Celia.

Ike stroked his beard. "Well, I got my dogs. O' course, they can't cook my beans, or chop wood...I been thinkin' maybe I'll get me a woman. A good hard-workin' woman, with a little meat on her bones. Them skinny ones allus has the coldest feet."

"Maybe a woman wouldn't like it here," suggested Celia, contemplating Ike's beard, his horse-colored underwear, the trickle of tobacco juice at the corner of his mouth. "And maybe a woman might make you do things — like shaving, putting in a bathroom, burning all your old clothes."

"Nope," growled Ike. "The woman I get me, she won't throw no weight around. One holler outa her, and she'll think twice about the next time."

Milo laughed. "Maybe she'd leave you."

"Ho ho!" crowed Ike. "Not much! When I gets me a woman, she stays got. You won't chase her away with a harpoon!"

Celia restrained a grin. "Well, I hope that when you find a woman you like, you can persuade her to come out here to live."

"No danger to that," said Ike. "That's the simplest part." He looked her up and down. "Now you, you looks like maybe you'd make a good worker. Might be you'd like to move in?"

"I think not." Celia took Milo's hand.

"Well, that just goes to show you," said Ike. "Now if you had jest a *leetle* more flesh on you, I'd start workin' —" Ike winked broadly "— and before long you'd be follerin' me around." He spat reflectively. "But I think I'll wait a bit, git me more what I got my mind on."

"Well," said Celia, her voice quivering, "I'm just as pleased."

"That's as may be." Ike turned away. "Got to feed the dogs."

Milo asked, "When are you going after your whales?"

Ike turned amber eyes in his direction. "What's it to you, son?"

"Nothing at all," said Milo, flushing. "Just curiosity."

"Maybe tomorrow, maybe the next day — when the signs are right." He turned away once more.

"Goodbye," said Celia.

"So long," said Milo.

Ike waved a hand and strode off toward his dogs.

Chapter VII

Bird Island Hotel was once again open to the public, and a grand banquet signaled the occasion. Fougasse insisted on a formal ten-course dinner, declaring that anything less elegant not only reflected upon Coves, the Bird Island Hotel, and Fougasse's professional repute, but injured Fougasse's personal self-esteem. "For the hunt lunch, Monsieur, yes," he cried in agitation. "For the buffet, the casual picnic, a want of the niceties is admissible. For the formal dinner — when that is directed by Fougasse — correctness is *de rigueur*, *cela s'entend*, all remaining possibilities must instantly be dismissed. Reflect, M. Coves, would you serve portions of ensilage to your guests? No? Oatmeal porridge? No? Tinned sardines? No? Then, in all logic, Monsieur, why halt to the side of perfection?"

Coves found no choice but to agree, though he had not envisioned so elaborate an affair. But by degrees he absorbed Fougasse's enthusiasm, and Fougasse, tapping his teeth with the point of a long pencil and taking quick strides about the kitchen, delivered himself while Coves sagely nodded his head.

"For the excellent dinner," said Fougasse, "I may say, Monsieur, it is necessary to conceive with the subtlety of the artist. Nothing may be omitted, and reckless departure from the precepts of the masters can lead but to bathos and *gaucherie*. So, M. Coves, now to the problem. We have the chef, we have the occasion, we have the victualing. M. Coves, as a man of discrimination, what is your idea as to this dinner?"

Coves rubbed his chin. "Well, to begin with, of course we ought to have a soup —"

"Exactly!" exclaimed Fougasse. "Preceded — as you say — by

an oyster or two. Now for the pattern I have in mind, the soup, M. Coves, should be a crafty *Julienne Faubonne*. You are familiar with the preparation? No? *N'importe*, your assistance will not be required. We will select for this occasion the fine Julienne, quenelles for the garnish. Do you agree, M. Coves?"

Coves said, "I'm sure that will be very nice, M. Fougasse."

"Then that is our decision," said Fougasse, tapping his teeth. Abruptly: "To work! Much remains. You have decided wisely. Duckling *à la bourguignonne* it shall be, with a good red Burgundy. We may serve a Volnay, or another Côte de Beaune. Then a bit of cheese, a bite of apple, a nectarine, a grape…Coffee and liqueurs…M. Coves, it might be well to inspect your cellar in regard to the necessary wines, cordials, and liqueurs."

Coves scratched his cheek with a sheepish forefinger. "Well, Mr. Fou — M. Fougasse, the bar supplies are in the cabinet — whisky, gin, brandy — things like that. Perhaps I've neglected the wines and liqueurs —"

"*Ciel!*" exclaimed Fougasse. "And a banquet is to exist? M. Coves, we must find the worst at once!" He stormed through the lobby, pushed through into the bar, where a small and elderly bartender in a sand-colored toupee was unpacking glasses from cartons and arranging them on shelves.

"I think there's an invoice," said Coves feebly. "You can look that over…Ah, here it is."

Fougasse seized it. He ran his eye along the items, an expression of scorn twisting his lips.

"Pah!" He glanced at Coves and the apprehensive bartender. "The barest rudiments, the complete inadequacy! How could a single meal be served? Monsieur, it is laughable. We must repair the situation in haste…I will mention the barest outline for civilized cuisine." He seized a bit of paper and scribbled faster than he spoke:

"To the liqueurs: Noyaux, Prunelle, Crème de Menthe —"

"We have Crème de Menthe," interposed Coves.

"— Crème Yvette, Kummel, Danziger Goldwasser, Kirsch, Curaçao, Maraschino, Bénédictine, Chartreuse —"

"There's some Chartreuse, too," said Coves eagerly.

Fougasse raised his eyes slowly at this second interruption. "You claim to have Chartreuse on the premises, M. Coves?"

Coves, not perceiving Fougasse's glittering dark eyes, turned to the bartender. "Ernest, hand me the Chartreuse."

The bartender presently set before them a squat bottle. This Fougasse seized, read the blue, red and white label. "Old Paragon Chartreuse." He repeated the words slowly, as if enjoying the rhythm of the syllables. "Old...Paragon...Chartreuse." He motioned to the bartender. "A glass."

He poured himself a finger of Old Paragon Chartreuse, lifted it to his lips, tasted. "M. Coves," said Fougasse gently, "you have been gulled and cheated. I urge that you sue this despicable wine merchant at a court of law, charging the most corrupt and flamboyant misrepresentation imaginable." He made another notation upon his list. "That will suffice, until we are able to advance to a more comprehensive selection."

Coves picked up the list, turned a wan gaze on Fougasse.

"You want these, *all* these wines?"

Fougasse made an eloquent gesture.

"But the expense!" moaned Coves. "There's a thousand dollars' worth of wine there, if I only bought two bottles of each!"

Fougasse shrugged. "A man employed at the delivery of mail must not begrudge the cost of shoes."

Coves reluctantly picked up the list. "I'll order them. I suppose if I make a point of it, they'll be here tomorrow."

"Almost too late," sighed Fougasse. "A wine should tranquilize after a journey, a month or more. Yet we will deal with the situation as well as possible."

At this moment Coves was called away to the lobby. Fougasse, a glance over his shoulder at the Old Paragon Chartreuse, departed for his own province.

The banquet, when at last it occurred, proved an enormous success, and Coves received numerous compliments — some of these from people whose opinions were to be respected. Coves' nephew held a post in a travel agency, and thus had been able to turn to Coves not a few distinguished guests, among them the eccentric philanthropist,

Mr. James Colin Boyce; the polo-player of international reputation, Mr. Cecil Lissacutt; Mrs. Winslow Denstrie Sipe, resting at Bird Island Hotel after her separation from Edward Sipe, the bath-mat manufacturer. Also present was the aged and irascible Mrs. Pedro Charmington, with her equally aged and no less irascible parrot; also Mr. Craintree Bezemer, the socialite-explorer, and the so-called 'stormy petrel of the pulpit' — the Reverend Anthony Dowbrett. And Coves, observing the enthusiasm which greeted the creations of M. Fougasse, felt that the expenditures for wines and liqueurs had not been futile.

After the banquet, while the guests still sipped their coffee, there entered the lobby a large man in a suit of striking russet. He had a broad face, a twisted nose, an aggressive jaw. He carried a small patent-leather satchel which he banged on the desk.

"I want a room," said the newcomer.

"Well," Coves said carefully, "I'm afraid we're full up. If you'd phoned for a reservation —"

The newcomer thrust his nose almost against that of Coves. "Now look here —" At this moment, Rexie the cat chose to walk across the desk between them, and his fine elevated tail bisected the space between their noses.

"Git away from me, you black imp," roared the newcomer, giving Rexie a smart slap on the rump. Outraged, Rexie sprang to the floor.

"Here! Here! Here!" cried Coves. "Don't you dare lay a hand on that cat! I'll have you arrested!"

"Stow the gab and hustle me a good room," snarled the newcomer, "or I'll call the boss and have you fired."

"I happen to be the owner!" yelled Coves. "Get out of here —"

Mrs. Pedro Charmington came hobbling into the lobby, sucking the last traces of the duckling *Bourguignonne* from her lower plate. She was escorted by Mr. James Colin Boyce.

The newcomer leered at Coves. "How'd you like me to stand the fat guy on his head?"

"Why, I'll have you put in jail!" exclaimed Coves.

"The cops are a long way off," said his opponent. "By the time they got here, I could give everybody in the place a punch in the nose, duck the cook in his own dishwater — sic the cat onto the old lady's parrot,

— 44 —

and—see that good-lookin' piece slidin' into the room like a greased snake?" He referred to the elegant and fastidious Mrs. Winslow Denstrie Sipe. "You know what I'd do for her?"

"Oh!" moaned Coves. "If you don't go at once, I'll—"

"Okay, brother." The man squared his shoulders. "You asked for it!" He started firmly across the lobby for Mrs. Charmington, who was displaying the lace of her new shawl to Mr. Boyce.

"Wait!" cried Coves. "Come back here!" The man paused. "I think—I think there's a vacant room," mumbled Coves. "You can have that for tonight."

The man grinned. "I thought maybe you'd cough up."

"Sign here," said Coves. "That will be ten dollars."

The man signed. Coves leaned forward and read the card. "Joe Connolly."

"Address, please," he said coldly.

Tiger Joe Connolly gave Coves a sardonic glance, scribbled, "San Quentin, California."

"Oh my," said Coves. "Well…er, that will be ten dollars, please."

Tiger Joe picked up his suitcase. "What's eatin' you, brother? Do I look like the kind of a guy that ducks his hotel bills?"

Coves eyed the small patent-leather suitcase. He rang the bell. "Front!" The bellboy appeared. "Sam, take Mr.—Mr. Connolly to 243."

"Send up a pint of Old Crow," called Tiger Joe over his shoulder. "Put it on the bill."

Chapter VIII

Next morning, Tiger Joe Connolly awoke at ten-thirty, stretched his massive arms, yawned enormously, grunted, heaved himself out of bed. His toilet was stark and efficient. In five minutes he was prepared to face the world.

Coves was busy at the desk, with Rexie beside him washing his paws, when Tiger Joe came thudding down the steps. Coves glanced significantly at a man standing nearby smoking a cigar, cleared his throat determinedly.

"Mr. Connolly!"

Tiger Joe turned his face toward Coves. "Yeah, what's up?"

"I have your bill," said Coves. "I regret that I will be requiring your room."

Tiger Joe stepped ominously toward the desk. Rexie paused in the laving of his paws.

Coves, swaying back a trifle, tendered his bill.

"Your — your account, sir."

Tiger Joe swept up the paper, crushed it into a hard little ball. "Now," he said, "do you know what I'm gonna do with this bill? I'm gonna —"

Rexie sprang nimbly to the top of the mail cabinet and there — tucking his tail securely about his hind legs — calmly resumed the task of cleansing his paws, with an occasional insolent glance at Tiger Joe.

The burly man smoking a cigar sidled up to Tiger Joe. "Well, brother, what's the hitch?" His voice was like a horse walking through dry cornstalks.

Tiger Joe leered. The man opened his coat. The gleam of polished nickel escaped.

"This is Mr. Turk, the house detective," said Coves. "Mr. Turk, Mr. Connolly."

"Okay, brother," rasped Mr. Turk, "you got your bill." He put his hand suggestively into his coat pocket.

Tiger Joe's shoulders sagged a trifle. He looked down at the bill in his hand. "But — I wasn't planning to leave for a while."

"You heard what Mr. Coves said. So cough up, then blow. This ain't no hangout for yeggs."

"But — I ain't got any dough with me now," protested Tiger Joe. "I got a touch to make, then I'll be floating. In the meantime —" he turned back to Coves, tried to suffuse his countenance with wistful persuasiveness "— maybe you could find me a room?"

"You're not quite the class of trade I want," said Coves.

"Oh, I was just jokin' last night," said Tiger Joe.

"I'm no snob, Mr. Connolly," said Coves, "but you do bring down the tone of the establishment… That suit, unpressed, spotted —"

"I got another," said Tiger Joe eagerly.

"Those yellow shoes," winced Coves. "That tie —"

"I'll go up and change," offered Tiger Joe. "I got a nice tie, green with yellow arrows."

"Well," said Coves, "your mannerisms are offensive, your — ah, selection of terms." He glanced at Rexie, still staring lambently at Tiger Joe. "You even startled Rexie."

"Well — I didn't mean it."

"Don't think Rexie's feelings don't get hurt just like anybody else's," said Coves, "because they do."

Mr. Turk cleared his throat. "Throw the bum out, Mr. Coves, and —"

"Oh," said Tiger Joe, "is his name Rexie? By God, that's a smart-looking cat! Well, sure, I'm sorry if I scared him. I didn't mean nothing by it, naturally. Tchk — tchk — tchk — hey, Rexie, howsa boy?"

Tiger Joe nodded to Coves. "Yep, that's sure a fine figure of a cat. Nice coloring too. I don't know much about things like that — but I'd call that cat a — a — a poem of color. Yes sir."

Coves gazed fondly up at the perplexed Rexie. "Yes, I think he's rather handsome. He's got a well-shaped body — an excellent head."

"I'll bet his fur's as soft as — as soft!" marveled Tiger Joe. "Look at it shine!"

Mr. Turk snorted and flung himself into a nearby chair, where he sourly watched Coves and Tiger Joe discuss Rexie. And all the while, the vain Rexie preened and put himself through a series of attitudes on top of the mail cabinet.

Tiger Joe looked down at his bill, which he had quietly unfolded and smoothed. "Well," he sighed regretfully, "if you want me to leave — sure, I'll leave. But if you could find a room somewhere — anywhere, front or back — I'd sure appreciate it. And I'll have some dough in tonight."

"Well —" Coves hesitated. "Very well, Mr. Connolly. But you understand we don't tolerate any boisterous conduct — and those yellow shoes…"

"I'll change right now," said Tiger Joe, and he hastened upstairs to his room.

Mr. Turk came over to the desk. "Is he gonna stay on?"

Coves fiddled with the register. "Yes. I'll give him another chance. But at the first irregularity, out he goes."

Mr. Turk shrugged. He swung his eyes around the lobby. He had only arrived this morning, summoned by Coves' urgent demand to the employment agency, and Bird Island Hotel was still novel to him. "Of course, if it was me, I wouldn't clutter a nice place like this with hoods."

"Oh well," said Coves.

Mr. Turk strolled out on the terrace. Mrs. Winslow Denstrie Sipe, elegant and *soignée*, strolled into the lobby on the arm of Mr. Cecil Lissacutt, and Coves trotted over to ask if they were finding everything satisfactory.

In Room 243, Tiger Joe kicked off his yellow shoes, cursing Coves, Mr. Turk, Rexie the cat and Mrs. Charmington in as many breaths. He doffed his rust-colored suit, his red tie, and in their place assumed black shoes, a dark suit, the green tie with the yellow arrows — an ensemble he disliked exceedingly; in fact, it was the outfit issued him by the penitentiary at the time of his discharge. He gave his sparse hair a lick with the brush, glared at his reflection in the mirror, yanked open the door, stormed out into the passageway.

But it was a meek Tiger Joe who descended the staircase, a Tiger Joe quietly shod and suited; a Tiger Joe who nodded at Coves, stooped to pat Rexie, continued outside, and strode across the island. He panted up the slope to Milo's ridge, turned up toward the center of the island. The trees presently met him, surrounded, merged above him, and he passed onward through a pleasant land of prismatic green light, the smell of balsam and sappy wood, the occasional whistle of a bird. But Tiger Joe's mind was far away, and the landscape made little impact on his senses.

He crossed the plateau at the top of the mountain, started down the long opposite slope. Ten minutes later he stood before Mortimer Archer's house.

The door was locked. He knocked. Footsteps approached within, a little spy window slid open, a liquid brown eye looked forth. The eyelid quivered.

"Okay, Slippy," said Tiger Joe. "Open 'er up."

The window closed. Tiger Joe rapped again, then thumped with his fist. The knob turned, the door opened.

"Well, come on in, Joe," said Archer heartily. "Sure is good to see you. How did you ever locate me?"

Tiger Joe stepped swiftly forward. Archer tried to leap back. Tiger Joe swung an arm behind him, pinioning him. With his other hand he removed the little revolver from the pocket of Archer's robe. Then he released Archer.

Archer jerked his robe back into place, licked his lips. "What do you want? When did..." He stopped.

"When did I get out?" leered Tiger Joe. "Oh, a little bit back, Slippy. Took me a while to catch up with you. I made it, though...Got any cold beer? Hot walk over here."

Archer strode away to the kitchen, chewing at his neat mustache. Tiger Joe followed, stood in the doorway while Archer produced the beer. He let Archer precede him back to the living room. "Nice lay-out you got," said Tiger Joe. He contemptuously picked up a *Town and Country* from Archer's coffee table, flipped through the pages, tossed it back down, overturning a small porcelain mandarin. Archer raised his eyebrows in pain. Tiger Joe crossed the room, peered through an open doorway into the photographic studio.

"Still at the old racket, hey?" he asked jocularly.

Archer sipped his beer. "What do you want?"

"Well," said Tiger Joe, grinning, "I might be coming for what you owe me."

Archer set down his beer. "Let's get this straight. I don't owe you a cent."

Tiger Joe's leer became more pronounced. "I took the rap, didn't I? While you was living high on the rake-off? Well, I figure I got something coming on that."

Archer shrugged. "All of us took the same chance. You didn't make it. That doesn't give you any claim on me."

"Not even for my cut on the deal?"

"That's water over the bridge," said Archer. "I had to live. You were getting your board and room free — I wasn't."

Tiger Joe stared at Archer for several seconds, then took a gulp of beer. "One thing, Slippy, you still got your nerve."

Archer shrugged.

"How come you happened to locate here?" inquired Tiger Joe casually.

Archer made a vague gesture. "I got a good buy on the property. It's a quiet place for any little business I feel like handling."

"That all? You wouldn't be fooling a poor old jug-owl, would you, Slippy?"

Archer rose to his feet with an expression of humorous candor. "Well, Joe, I'll be perfectly frank with you. Remember Big Ben Manzio?"

"Sure I remember Big Ben Manzio."

"I heard that this was his island, and that he left a lot of boodle around here somewhere."

Tiger Joe sneered. "You expect me to believe that, Slippy?"

Archer shrugged. "Suit yourself."

"That's just what I'm doing," said Tiger Joe, relaxing into the seat. "We're partners again, Slippy. You owe me a lot. I could take it out of your hide and maybe I will. But I'd prefer taking it out of your pocketbook. If you're looking for Big Ben's loot, we'll look together. If it's something else — well, it's something else. 'Share and share alike'."

"Now look here," blustered Archer, "the day for that kind of stuff is over. I've put aside all my old associations, and that includes you. Where Manzio hid the stuff I don't know. If you can locate it, you're welcome to it, but you do it on your own. I've built up a front here, and I don't want you around to ruin it. I won't have —"

"Slippy," Tiger Joe said, "go get me another bottle of beer."

Archer met his gaze and the words he had been about to speak numbed in his mouth.

"You run the business, Slippy. You're in entire charge — because I know that whatever it is, you're making money at it, and a pretty stiff slug. No, the ideas — that's your job. Also the financing. Mine will be the rake-off."

There was a long silence. "Well, you got me where I can't argue with you," Archer said presently, and his voice had changed somewhat. "As a matter of fact, I can use some help."

"Attaboy, Slippy."

Archer appraised the massive form of his new associate. "Maybe you're just what the doctor ordered."

"What's the deal?"

"Well," said Archer, "it's like this. I have some friends who've been running bundles in from Mexico. Heroin mostly. The going's been pretty bad. The beard's got a clamp on the border, and about a month ago we lost a whole planeload, forced down over Arizona. Lost about three hundred grand, not counting the plane…Well, I happened to hear something interesting about this Bird Island here. It seems all the driftwood and floating junk in the ocean piles up on the beach. Some kind of trick of current."

"Ah," said Tiger Joe. "I'm startin' to get you."

"I made some tests. Numbered some bottles, took them out in a boat, threw 'em in at different spots, marking down on a chart where I dropped 'em. Then I waited till the bottles began appearing on the beach, and now I know pretty close just what'll happen when something's dropped into the ocean offshore."

"Sounds good," said Tiger Joe. "You figure to run a plane out, or a boat?"

"Either one. Whatever works out best. We'll ship out of Mexico,

Panama, South America — anywhere. Bring it to the area I've got charted, toss it overboard. The current does the rest."

Tiger Joe drank his beer thoughtfully. "Of course there's the hotel right along the beach. Somebody else might find it."

Archer laughed. "That's the angle we've got to work. We've got to take over the island."

"Yeah? How?"

Archer rose to his feet, strode back and forth. "We've got to scare 'em off, buy 'em off, or make it too expensive for 'em to stay. But we've got to do it in such a way that there won't be any suspicions, no law nosing around. In other words, we just can't liquidate everybody. Take Coves, for instance. Every cent he could lay his hands on he's got sunk in the hotel. If he has to spend any more money, or if he has a bum season, he won't be able to make ends meet. He'll go under, and we'll buy him out. And Green, up on the cliff. He's got his nose to the grindstone paying off his house. He'll be easy. There's an old coot from Alaska that's got some kind of pipe dream about whales. I don't know just yet how to handle him. And there's Ottenbright, next door to me. Maybe we could frame some scandal. Then there's the girls' school —"

"Hah!" said Tiger Joe, a gleam in his eye. "That's my department."

Archer shook his head. "We've got to do this careful, Joe. No rough stuff. We can't get people talking."

Tiger Joe said regretfully, "You got any ideas?"

"Lots of 'em." Archer leaned forward. "Listen…"

CHAPTER IX

8:00 A.M., WITH THE sun bright and yellow. Milo, in sand-colored shorts and Army shoes, worked his road down the ridge — digging, leveling, scraping, tamping.

Just ahead, an elbow of quartzite humped across the road, and Milo considered how best to defeat the obstacle. Should he fill in at either side, raising a hillock in the road? Or should he obliterate the barrier with dynamite? Perhaps the rock would yield to pick and sledge hammer. He exerted a few tentative blows and stood back, inspecting the terrain. But no other route was practical; the ridge at this point fell off on either side in steep, rocky steps. Milo shrugged his shoulders. There would have to be a hillock in his road. He laid down his shovel, wiped his hands on his shorts, and started for the house. After breakfast he would settle himself on the terrace with freshly sharpened pencils, pads of paper, a rhyming dictionary, and work till noon, composing verses for greeting cards. He had not abandoned his ballad, but the greeting card verses at least kept the house in groceries and might possibly make a dent in the bank payment.

At Miss Pickett's academy, the girls trooped out of the refectory, clean, neat, alert. Several, including Madeline Cheabrough, wore a sulky pout. Miss Pickett had forbidden lipstick, nail polish, bop records, jive talk and the cha-cha.

Celia was conducting her class in the history of music, and with great dignity confronting a group of girls only two or three years younger than herself, pretending she was as stern as her indomitable aunt. So far, no one had dared to challenge her.

Ike rose from his bunk at six o'clock, stretched, yawned, belched, pulled brown corduroy trousers up over his long undergarments. He slipped on his shoes, fired up his stove and set water to boil for coffee.

The rising sun beat in through the window like a bugle call. Ike shuffled to the window and looked out across the ocean. He blinked, nodded sagely to himself, scratched his beard. Pulling a mackinaw over his shoulders, he went out to his dogs. He fed them, filled their water pail, rubbed mange ointment on the back of Jupe. Wiping his fingers on a bit of burlap, he re-entered the cabin, cooked and ate his breakfast, reflecting as he did so that a woman around the camp could take the doctoring of the dogs off his hands, as well as performing various other duties.

At seven o'clock he sauntered down to the dock where his launch swung on the lazy swell. He loaded two five-gallon cans of gasoline on the floorboards, also some lard pails full of a viscous liquid. He started the engine, cast off, steered across the cove, through the gate in the barrier, which he took care to lash wide ajar. Then Ike set out to sea.

The day was fine, the sun warm, the motor of the launch ticked over like an expensive watch. Ike felt the urge toward music. First he hummed, then he broke into song — a ceremonial chant of the obscure Bakulchuk tribe. It was a ditty Ike would sing on his way home from trading fur for cornmeal, a new squaw and rye whiskey.

The launch became a black dot on the horizon, disappeared.

Four or five hours later the black dot appeared once more. This time it was followed by other hulking black forms, thirteen in all. Ike stood in the stern of the launch with a spoon, ladling gobs of the viscous liquid into the wake. Blowing, puffing, thrashing the water with their mighty flukes, the whales drifted forward, impelled by no visible agency.

Bird Island loomed close; the great semicircle of piles curved directly ahead. The gate stood open. Ike ran the launch through the gate, and after him came the whales.

Ike closed the gate, steered his launch to the dock, tied up. For an hour he stood watching while the whales drove angrily about the enclosure, battering at the piles. At last they lay sullenly on the surface, swirling the water behind them with sudden furious sweeps of their flukes.

Ike heaved a sigh. "Thirteen whale. Most meat I've ever had at one time... And all I got to do now is keep 'em clean of sucker-lice and barnacles."

Rexie sat on the desk beside the register, and beside him Coves busily tended his bookkeeping.

A great figure suddenly appeared around the corner of the desk: Tiger Joe Connolly. Rexie flattened his ears, backed against the wall, spat defiantly. Tiger Joe bent over him. "Howsa little pussy today? Nice kitty, purty kitty." He reached out and stroked Rexie's head.

"That's sure a purty cat, Mr. Coves," said Tiger Joe. "Almost wish I owned him."

An indulgent smile touched Coves' lips. "Yes, Rexie's all right."

Rexie relaxed a trifle.

Tiger Joe spied Mrs. Pedro Charmington hobbling across the lobby, and bounded forward to offer his arm. Coves noted that Tiger Joe was almost correctly dressed in a new suit of herringbone tweed, two-toned shoes, a blue sports shirt with collar tabs the size and shape of falcon's wings.

Fougasse appeared at Coves' elbow, leading a sullen Mario.

"M. Coves, I must beg that you do not mingle in the kitchen arrangements! Tonight the brioche paste must be executed, and this buffoon informs me that you have permitted him the evening away!"

Coves glanced from one to the other. "Why, I told him it was all right with me, if you gave him permission."

"And I asked you," burst out Mario. "It was this morning — and you said yes, yes, anything, so long as I got out the eggs without clouding the yolks. Eggs Monaco, it was."

Fougasse strode back and forth. "It is unthinkable! With the brioche paste to prepare? Who then is to knead! Charles? He is engaged with the *foie-gras* rissoles. I? M. Coves? No less impossible. M. Mario, I will not have it! The brioche must *marche*!"

Mario shrugged despairingly, turned away to the kitchen.

Fougasse sighed. "The folly of that one's nature. Have you heard the latest? Cloves in the *Chicken portugais*! I must watch his every move."

Coves shook his head sympathetically.

"Also, M. Coves, where are the ortolans? I order them the day before yesterday and they have not arrive'. What am I to do?" Fougasse extended his hands expressively. As a matter of fact, Coves, discovering the price of a two-ounce ortolan, and fearing waste if the dish proved unpopular, had deleted the item.

"Perhaps we could have a few nice squabs, instead," suggested Coves hopefully. "I really don't think the ortolans would go over well. They're so expensive — and they might go to waste."

"Waste?" scoffed Fougasse. "Nonsense! If no one else, I, Fougasse, would eat them, every one!" Fougasse stared blankly across the lobby, massaging his supple face. "*Ah tiens*! There is no doubt an oversight. Tonight I will repeat the demand, and the ortolans will surely arrive at once."

Coves made a mental note to intercept the order. Fougasse leaned upon the desk. "M. Coves, I note that under the lobby exists a considerable aperture."

"Oh yes. That's where the slope falls away underneath."

"I have investigated," announced Fougasse. "I find it cool, dark, well-aired but not draughty. In short, I fancy the region would provide a magnificent cheesery."

"'Cheesery'?"

"Cheesery? Is not that the expression? Where one makes cheese? No matter. We set aside the curd, mingling therein a culture found only at Montdembois on the Loire. And in not too long a time you shall smack your lips over a most savory cheese."

"Of course, Mr. Fougasse, do whatever you like. Er, there won't be any smell?"

"Smell? Pah! Fragrance, one should say! However, Monsieur, do not fear; the odor emanates horizontally, never in a vertical mode — a peculiarity of the Montdembois."

"I see," said Coves. "Well certainly, Mr. Fougasse, go right ahead."

Fougasse returned to the kitchen, and Coves returned to his figures. A tendril of musky redolence pulled at his nostrils like a crochet hook. Coves looked up. "Why, good morning, Mrs. Sipe."

The regal divorcée approached the desk.

"Good morning, Mr. Coves. Tell me, have you seen Mr. Lissacutt anywhere?"

"Why no, Mrs. Sipe, I haven't."

The lady shook her head, frowning. "How infinitely tiresome! He promised to take me to the summit of the hill."

"Good morning, Mr. Coves," said the young man who had just wandered into the lobby — a pleasant-looking chap with tousled brown hair and serious blue eyes.

"Why hello, Mr. Green," said Coves cordially. "Glad to see you. Er — Mrs. Sipe, Mr. Green."

"How do you do?" said Milo.

"Mr. Green lives in the house on the crag," explained Coves.

Mrs. Sipe's manner became a degree less impersonal. "Your view must be simply breath-taking, Mr. Green." She reached into her handbag for her gold cigarette case.

"Excuse me," said Milo. "Have one of mine."

"No, thank you." Mrs. Sipe favored him with a quick smile. "I smoke nothing but my own brand. They're made by a little shop I discovered in Istanbul." She placed the ivory cylinder to her lips, and Coves held up a match.

Mrs. Sipe turned, leaned her elegant back against the desk, and surveyed the lobby. "Well, it's evident that I am abandoned." She turned Coves an arch glance. "When you see Mr. Lissacutt, reprimand him without mercy... And the hillside seems so pleasant this morning."

"I'd be glad to be of assistance," said Milo.

"Mr. Green, you're very kind! I'm simply aching to wander around the island — but of course I couldn't impose upon you..."

"Why not?" asked Milo. "When would you like to go?"

"I'll just run up, slip into a pair of walking shoes and be right back." She smiled glowingly at Coves, walked across the lobby, hips oscillating in an ample, fluid orbit.

"That's very nice of you, Mr. Green," said Coves. "I'm sure you'll enjoy your walk. Mrs. Sipe is a cultured woman, very charming — a real woman of the world." Coves lowered his voice to a confidential pitch. "She had a breakdown during her last divorce; that's why she's here, resting."

Mrs. Sipe returned in her walking costume — lavender-gray skirt, with a darker lavender fur-trimmed jacket. She carried a gay orange scarf, printed with red Eiffel towers and French phrases, and wore low-heeled brown alligator brogues.

"Now, Mr. Green, shall we start?"

It was indeed a pleasant morning, and they slowly mounted the central ridge, Mrs. Sipe turning now and again to remark at the beauty of the vista, declaring that it reminded her of nothing more than the Dalmatian coast near Spalato.

They reached the summit. A man sitting on a rock nearby with a pair of binoculars in his lap arose. It was Mortimer Archer, dapper in tweed trousers, a sports jacket of British cut, a flannel cap.

"Good morning," said Archer, placing the binoculars in their case. "Taking the air, eh, Green? Haven't had the pleasure of seeing you for several weeks."

"No," Milo admitted, "I've been keeping close to home. Mrs. Sipe, this is Mr. Archer. Mr. Archer, Mrs. Sipe."

"And you're another lucky inhabitant of the island?" asked Mrs. Sipe.

Mr. Archer nodded. "My house is over the hill, down the slope. I doubt if you can see it from here. Just a modest little place — more studio than anything else."

"Ah," cried Mrs. Sipe. "I thought so! The moment I saw you I said 'artist'. What is your medium, Mr. Archer? Or let me guess…Now I should say," she tapped her chin with a fingernail, "oils. Yes, you're definitely the type. Now tell me I'm right."

Archer laughingly shook his head. "I'm afraid not. At least not at the moment. I've given up oils; I'm concentrating on photography."

"How interesting!" murmured Mrs. Sipe. "I'd love to see your work. I'm sure that if your studies reflect this Arcadian environment, they must be great things."

"Nature is the true artist," said Archer modestly. "I merely find its beauties, capture the impression on film."

"But," Mrs. Sipe pointed out, "that is the art — the seeing, the perceiving of the composition. The oil painter might in the same way deprecate his art, declaring that the colors were there, all he did was to place them on the canvas. No, Mr. Archer, art is art, no matter what the medium."

Archer shrugged. "I hope you won't change your mind when you've seen my work."

Mrs. Sipe shook her finger. "Mr. Archer, your modesty must be affected. But tell me, who else shares the island with you and Mr. Green and Mr. Coves?"

"Miss Pickett runs a school for young ladies. Over the hill there's Mr. Ottenbright, a San Francisco attorney, and a rather eccentric old character, Ike O'Rourke, who runs what he calls a 'whale farm'."

"A 'whale farm'?"

"Yes, he's captured a number of whales, though what he intends to do with them I'm sure I don't know. I think that if we walk over this way, we might actually be able to look down at this 'whale farm'."

"How utterly fascinating!" exclaimed Mrs. Sipe.

They crossed the little tableland, and Archer halted. "Let's see — this ravine runs down into the cove where Ike pens his whales." He indicated the gully below them, where a little stream raced down to the ocean.

Chatting gaily, the three started down the ravine. "'Hoy!" came a cry to their left. "Hold up, thar!"

"Why, it's Ike himself," Archer whispered to Mrs. Sipe. "You'll be amused."

Ike came sauntering down from the height to their left. As usual, he wore his brown corduroy trousers, with underwear displayed leadenly to the sight of all.

"My word," whispered Mrs. Sipe, "what a quaint old fellow! I marvel at those whiskers! But isn't he a little — well, a little —"

"Oh, entirely," whispered Archer.

"Whereabouts you three headin'?" called Ike.

"We were trying to glimpse your famous whale farm, Mr. O'Rourke," replied Archer. "Excuse me, Mrs. Sipe, may I present Mr. O'Rourke?"

"Call me Ike, lady." He turned back to Archer. "I'm just lookin' around, maybe to put signs up: 'No Trespassing, Beware of Shotgun'."

"What on earth for?" gasped Mrs. Sipe. "Do sight-seers disturb your whales?"

"I don't know as you'd call 'em sight-seers, lady. There's a lot of money in them whales. I aim to shoot first and ask questions afterwards. What I really needs is an assistant." He inspected Mrs. Sipe appraisingly, stepped to the side for a better view of her silhouette.

"Say, lady," declared Ike, "dang if you ain't a right spankin' smart woman."

Archer stiffened. "Why, really, Mr. O'Rourke —"

Ike ignored him. "You married, lady?"

"I am not," was the cold reply.

"You any hand at grindin' up pemmican?"

"Certainly not!" declared Mrs. Sipe.

"Ever cure any hides?"

"I'm afraid we must be going," said Mrs. Sipe frigidly. "Good day, Mr. O'Rourke."

"Wait now, don't be huffy," said Ike. "I was just askin'. Anyways, it's easy to learn."

"What is that peculiar odor?" inquired Mrs. Sipe of Milo. "It's like a mixture of…" Delicately she groped for words; and with equal restraint Milo refrained from pointing out that the wind blew from Ike.

"Well, we must be leaving," said Mrs. Sipe. "I'm dreadfully thirsty." She glanced at the little stream running past their feet down the ravine. "I wonder if that water is good to drink?"

"Why, it certainly is," said Ike affably. "Here, I've got a little tin cup. I'll rinse it out, and in a minute you'll have the coolest, freshest drink of your life." He reached in his pocket, pulled out a collapsible aluminum cup, turned his back, filled the cup, handed it to Mrs. Sipe.

"Wonderful!" declared the divorcée. "Nothing is as delicious as spring water!"

"Go ahead," said Ike. "Drink it all. Water's sweet and cold." He turned, glared at Archer and Milo. "You two stay back there till after the lady drinks. You'll muddy the water. Mind now!" He scowled so fiercely that Milo and Archer drew back.

"Delicious," murmured Mrs. Sipe, drinking. "Ah…" She stood rigid, quivering.

Ike said, "Still thirsty, dearie?" A grin moved his whiskers.

"No — thank you," said Mrs. Sipe, in a faraway voice.

"Now then, dearie, here's old Ike, who's looking for a good woman —"

And the astounded Archer and Milo heard Mrs. Sipe say, "But darling, I'm here, you know."

"I reckon you'll do all right," said Ike, and Mrs. Sipe flung herself into his arms.

"What on earth —" sputtered Archer.

"You two git," said Lonesome Ike. "Me and the little lady want to be alone."

"Darling," Mrs. Sipe turned to Ike, "it's so strange — I've never realized what a helpless creature I am! Why, I don't even know how to cook pemmican!"

"You don't cook it," said Ike. "You sucks it. Jerky, you chews on it. It's cornmeal you cooks."

"But I've found you, and all that will be changed. I felt it in my bones the minute I saw you! Oh, I've never been so thrilled!"

"Mrs. Sipe," inquired Milo in alarm, "are you all right? Can I —"

"Look here, young fellow," said Ike good-naturedly, "you leave the lady be. She's made up her mind —"

"Oh, indeed I have," sighed Mrs. Sipe.

"Would you like a drink of cold water?" Milo asked anxiously.

"Enough's enough," said Ike. "Leave well enough alone." He turned to Mrs. Sipe. "Well, come on, old lady, let's get on home. I'll put on a shirt, maybe wash up a leetle, and we'll run across to town and git hitched up proper."

"Darling!" breathed Mrs. Sipe.

"But Mrs. Sipe," cried Milo as she turned to go, "do you know what you're doing?"

Mrs. Sipe's haughty stare chilled Milo. "Mr. Green, you forget your manners." She turned her elegant back, hooked her arm through that of Ike, and they swept off down the ravine.

Milo started after them, then halted, staring.

"Interesting episode," murmured Archer, chewing at his mustache.

"What shall I tell Coves?"

Archer shrugged. "Tell him that Ike and Mrs. Sipe met, and decided to be married."

"Well," said Milo dubiously, "inasmuch as that, broadly speaking, is exactly what happened…"

CHAPTER X

SHORTLY AFTER ONE O'CLOCK. The guests, rendered torpid by Fougasse's craft, sat in various languid poses along the terrace. Within, Coves made entries in his ledger.

A figure entered the lobby and moved slowly to the magazine rack, became absorbed in the titles. Coves, with his deerlike sensitivity to psychic tension, glanced up, then, laying aside his pen, hurried across the lobby. Rexie marched closely at his heels.

"Good afternoon, Mr. Green," said Coves.

"Hello, Mr. Coves."

"I hope you had a nice stroll?"

"Very."

"I imagine Mrs. Sipe enjoyed herself?"

"Yes...I suppose you'd say she did...That was my impression, at least."

"I didn't see her come in. She's out on the terrace, I presume?"

"I don't think so," said Milo. "The fact is..." His voice trailed off.

"Where *is* Mrs. Sipe, Mr. Green?"

"Well," said Milo, "the fact is, we met Mr. Archer and Mr. O'Rourke at the top of the hill. We talked for a while; then Mrs. Sipe and Mr. O'Rourke decided that they wanted to be married, and so Mr. Archer and I —" he carefully inspected his fingertips "— left them alone, and I came back to tell you that she'll probably be moving out."

As Coves tottered backward, he stepped on Rexie's tail. Rexie screeched and fled. Coves sank into a chair. Step by step, Milo explained the morning's events.

For a considerable period Rexie brooded, then deciding that a walk through the meadow would relieve his melancholy, he rose to his feet.

The lobby was quiet. Milo had left for his home on the crag, Coves had retired to his room. Rexie ran out the French doors, across the terrace, around the building, and into the grass.

The grass was delightful, full of small soothing noises when the wind blew, and Rexie sauntered back and forth along the sweet-smelling aisles. The sunlight shone through the bladed screen, threw a tiger pattern on Rexie's fur... Ah! The scent of mouse? To be sure, and there he ran, scuttling ahead! Rexie leapt forward gracefully. Look, the foolish creature was leaving the grass, running toward the terrace! An addled mouse indeed! Rexie increased his pace. The mouse flung himself around the corner of the terrace, escaping Rexie by an inch. Rexie gathered himself, dashed around the corner... He dug his claws into the red flagstones; they scraped as he frantically braked himself. The mouse had become a fiend, a monster! Rexie vented an appalling scream and fled madly for the darkest, most secret recesses under the hotel.

Mr. Craintree Bezemer, the socialite explorer, loved to excite sensation. To this end he could always rely upon the presence of his pet baboon, past whom Rexie's mouse had darted. When he answered questions, Mr. Bezemer practiced a careful modesty.

"Yes, Banjo is the gift of Batongo, chief of the Pulu Tribe — darkest, deepest Africa, of course. I had an opportunity to do him a trifling service, though I doubt if the lion would have caught him in any event. And he really made a tremendous pother over the fact that I only had my light revolver... Anyway, he insisted that I take Banjo. And rather than offend the old blighter, I took him. We've become quite attached. Quite an intelligent beast..."

Miss Pickett's academy always had been prosperous. Unlike Mr. Coves, she ran her establishment with Doric austerity. Her creed was that simple food and sober clothing made for a harder fiber of woman, and in most cases the parents of her pupils agreed. "Daughter is, of course, a dear sweet thing," they would say, "but she's had so much all her life that a little simplicity and discipline will do wonders for her."

These were almost the exact words used by Mrs. Cheabrough in connection with a letter from Madeline.

Mummy, darling,

Life goes on as usual, and I wish you'd get me away from here. Do you think I'm training for one of those convents where the nuns wear burlap and eat nothing but turnips? What utter stark want! For breakfast, oatmeal and eggs, and toast. For lunch, creamed tuna and spinach. For dinner, lima beans and hash. Dessert? What's that? Miss Pickett thinks sweet stuff is bad for girls. And we don't get any spending money as a result of that awful agreement you made with Miss Pickett.

(Miss Pickett, at the beginning of the term, requested that no spending money be provided the students, this to prevent indulgence in sweets, and also to discourage the formation of cliques.)

So here we sit, me with my tongue down to my collarbone for a milkshake, and what do I get? Iced tea. I'm practically desperate. One thing about Miss Pickett's system, it certainly develops resourcefulness, and J. B. Carr and Skippy Ballard and I have developed a source of revenue. It should keep us in as much unwholesome candy and cigarettes as the heart would desire.

Everybody's afraid of Miss Pickett. Not that she does anything mean; it's just her manner. She has a Presence, no question as to that. She glides around like a wraith, but the skin at the back of your neck always lets you know when she's near. Her niece, Celia Marlowe, is a darling, however. She's exquisitely lovely — everybody's jealous of her — but she's moody. I think Miss Pickett suppresses her. Or else she's in love. Or both. If one of the last two, everybody knows who it is: Milo Green, who has a nice dreamy look to him. He lives in that house up on top the hill. He's a writer or something. I'd like to land him myself.

Nothing else of excitement. Miss Pickett lets us have visitors Friday and Saturday evenings, but we can't go ashore on dates because the launch doesn't run after six.

Love,
Madeline

Mrs. Cheabrough folded the letter, observed to her sister, "I guess Miss Pickett rather puts the girls through it. But it'll do Madeline good to run up against somebody she can't wheedle."

"I wonder what Madeline means when she says she has a 'source of revenue'?"

Mrs. Cheabrough sniffed. "She probably has some little racket. There's bound to be money somewhere in the group, and there's bound to be girls like Madeline smart enough to get it away from whomever has it."

Ike leaned in the doorway counting his whales. The new Mrs. O'Rourke was visible behind him, washing the dinner dishes.

"Yup," said Ike. "All I need now is just hold what I got till the renderin' ship comes by. Look at 'em!" And he spat reverently. "Whales, whales, whales!"

Mrs. Winslow Denstrie Sipe O'Rourke looked over his shoulder. "Darling, isn't it marvelous? And all of them ours!"

Ike spat once more. "Darling," exclaimed Mrs. O'Rourke, "not among the petunias! And I'll mend that underwear for you if you'd only take it off."

Ike regarded her coldly. "Take 'em off? Why, woman, you like to get me down with pneumony and kill me off?"

"Darling!" gasped Mrs. O'Rourke. "Don't talk like that!"

Ike contentedly resumed the counting of his whales.

Mortimer Archer stood at the tank in his darkroom, washing film. His skin was pallid, his mustache natty, his eyes as spaniel-like as ever — but his look of overcivilized indolence had vanished. He was deft and intent; his hands moved competently.

He held the negative to the dim red light. A beautiful shot — worth two or three hundred dollars... The doorbell rang. Archer dropped the negative into a basin, peeled off his rubber gloves.

The peephole showed him a gnarled cheek, an oblique jaw, an ear like wadded chewing gum. Archer opened the door. Tiger Joe sauntered in.

"Well, Slippy, how's business?"

"Pretty good."

Tiger Joe went to the middle of the room, looked up, down, back, forth. Archer watched from near the door, hands in the pockets of his robe. Tiger Joe completed his scrutiny of the room, turned back to Archer. "What's new?"

Archer wordlessly opened a drawer, tossed an envelope to Tiger Joe. Tiger Joe pulled out six photographs.

"Woo! Slippy, I got to hand it to you. These is the magoo…Where they going?"

"So far, a thousand sets to Chicago, a thousand to Los Angeles, a thousand to Reno, five hundred to Fort Worth, New Orleans and Miami. That's just small-time stuff. I'll hear from the Eastern agent in a day or two. Then I sold a set to one of the magazines."

Tiger Joe nodded. "That's right, Slippy. Work the angles, make money for the company."

Archer tossed the photographs into a drawer.

"What have you been doing?" There was a sardonic overtone in his voice which Tiger Joe, who had gone to the kitchen for a bottle of beer, did not catch.

"Everything's under control. The old buckaroo's got a gang of whales, all right. I'll fix that wagon pretty soon. He's got hisself a rich widder, what's he want with more loot?"

"How's business at the hotel?"

"Booming. He ain't got enough room to hold everybody. But as soon as I think of something real good, I'll settle him; also the old snipe that runs the girls' school. That should be easy. And then we'll scare off the punk up on the hill — Green."

Archer smiled thinly. "Maybe yes, maybe no. Maybe he won't scare."

Tiger Joe tilted the bottle, took a great gurgling swallow. He wiped his mouth. "No sense in taking chances, that's a cinch. I suppose I could cool him once and for all."

Archer shook his head. "He'll probably go back on his bank loan and we'll take over the equity."

"It might throw a scare in the rest of the gang," Tiger Joe put forward thoughtfully.

Archer shook his head a second time. "Everything's got to go quietly; we can't stand advertisement." After a moment he said casually, "Another thing, I know how to handle old lady Pickett. No fuss, no nothing. Foolproof."

"What's the angle?"

Archer leaned forward. "I was going to keep it to myself, but it's too rich. Do you know how O'Rourke got that woman of his?"

"No," said Tiger Joe in sudden interest. "I been wondering." He straightened in his chair. "Dirty old geezer, a high-class twist like that. She wouldn't even give me a tumble."

"I wouldn't believe it if I hadn't seen it myself," said Archer. "I ran into him down along the shore the other day, got the inside dope. It seems the Eskimos make some kind of stuff out of boiled-down polar bear—" He reached into his pocket, displayed an aspirin bottle half-full of a murky liquid. "I talked him into giving me a little. He's got about a gallon of the stuff."

Tiger Joe sat back in his chair. "What's the dose?"

"A little better than a drop and a half, according to O'Rourke."

Chapter XI

Dᴜʀɪɴɢ ᴛʜɪꜱ ᴘᴇʀɪᴏᴅ Rᴇxɪᴇ found only one real solace: Fougasse's cheese cellar. When overcome by frustration or gloom, Rexie could always creep to this dim sanctum under the hotel, and there eat cheese. When expecting a coarse epithet and a spank from Tiger Joe, but instead receiving praise and tickling behind the ears; or when on the other hand he would run joyously forward in greeting, only to be met with curses and a blow; then Rexie in his bafflement would flee under the hotel and eat cheese.

Each encounter with Tiger Joe left his head swimming. And day after day, covertly watching the baboon, Rexie asked himself when it would resume its ordinary mouse-like form.

It was Rexie's custom, about 10:00 P.M., to stroll into the bar where Ernest the bartender would serve him a dish of pure cream. In accordance with this habit he trotted briskly in from the lobby, mouth watering in anticipation. A florid middle-aged guest with a mop of white hair sat at the bar drinking a milk punch, and at this man's insistence Ernest the bartender, in place of the cream, poured Rexie some milk punch and set the saucer in its usual place.

Rexie leapt to a stool, then to the bar, lowered his head. Several mouthfuls passed down his throat before he noticed the peculiar flavor of the liquid. He paused, stared into the saucer with narrowed eyes. The liquid, so his eyes told him, was cream. Rexie had never known a white liquid which was not milk or cream. Obviously the liquid was cream... Rexie lapped up every drop in sheer defiance.

Presently Rexie became aware of a tingling in his throat, a pleasant lightness to his feet. He twitched his tail several times vigorously.

At this moment Mr. Craintree Bezemer brought his baboon into the bar.

Rexie spied the pseudo-mouse, and his tail tautened instantly. Ah, here was the false creature again! Up to his old tricks, eh? Rexie, full of Dutch courage, flexed his muscles.

Narrowly he inspected the baboon, and sat back momentarily perplexed. This hallucination was so much larger than the mouse it concealed that it became a problem at which end to jump. If he leapt for the forequarters, the mouse might be lurking near the tail, and so escape. Or if he chose to spring at the tail, the mouse, if situated in the region delineated by the foreparts, might likewise win free.

Rexie compromised. He crouched, quivered an instant, launched himself directly at the middle of the beast.

Instead of sailing right through nothingness to grasp a mouse, Rexie met hard ribs and ill-smelling hide.

A whirlwind tussle of squalling baboon and equally vehement Rexie ensued — up and down, over and under, the baboon yanking at Rexie, stamping on him; Rexie, ears laid back, climbing up the short-furred back, biting and scratching. The baboon cuffed Rexie, and Rexie sprang free, raced from the bar, through the lobby, and into the most inaccessible region under the hotel.

Rexie's behavior worried Coves. "I don't understand it at all," he said to Milo in the lobby. "He jumps at the slightest noise. Yesterday he even spat at Mr. Connolly, which he's never done before."

"Sounds like indigestion," said Milo.

Coves shook his head. "I doubt it. Another thing: in the encounter with Mr. Bezemer's baboon he received a small cut on the neck. I've put salve and antiseptic on it, but it just doesn't seem to heal. I wonder if you'd look at it and tell me if you think it's infected?"

Milo shrugged. "Sure I'll look at him."

The reluctant Rexie was captured and exhibited. Milo inspected the sore.

"Do you think it's serious?" Coves asked.

"Hard to say," said Milo. "I had a dog with a place like that once, and I put peroxide on it. Seemed to help it heal."

"Hydrogen peroxide?"

"That's right. And maybe a light bandage to keep him from licking it."

Coves nodded his comprehension and hurried away with Rexie.

So the days passed on Bird Island. Golden mornings, hazy afternoons, velvet nights — and life moved almost as in a dream. Only Milo Green exhibited traits of doubt and despondency.

Late one afternoon he sailed his boat to Larkspur, collected his mail, searched through the envelopes, gleaned a handful of small checks.

Returning toward the dock, he passed the Roisterers' Club. He glanced at his watch. Time for a beer. He entered, took a seat at the bar, where — over his fourth highball — he fell into a discussion with a man who was convinced that snails could produce pearls as efficiently as oysters if trained to the task. An hour later Milo had switched to a drink he called a Roman Holiday and was expounding the theory of the mixture to his friend.

Two hours later, the man's wife appeared and led him away.

Milo decided to leave also. Gaining his feet, he left the Roisterers' Club and continued toward the dock.

Evening had surrendered to night, and Milo, peering up and down the dock, found it difficult to distinguish the bow of his boat from the stern. Eventually he blundered into the stern, and the craft remained upright only because Milo had fallen flat on his face.

With exquisite care Milo turned himself over, lifted an arm, hoisted the sail, pulled himself aft to the rudder. The breeze filled the sail, the boat heeled, Milo slumped drunkenly to windward. Some time later Milo found that he had not yet cast free of the dock.

At last he won loose and the boat plunged swiftly for Bird Island. Foam bubbled at the bow, vanished palely aft.

Halfway across the wind died. Milo glared resentfully into the darkness. The sail flapped limply. Cursing, Milo searched for his paddle, only to remember that five minutes previously he had flung it at a swooping bird of the night. And now the current took hold, swept the craft out past Point Lobos in the direction of the Galapagos Islands.

Timeless, windless darkness. Rising, falling in empty black vastness, and Milo with a spinning head. Island and mainland were a black loom together, far behind. A high midnight overcast hid the stars.

The breeze came to life as quickly as it had died. Bringing the boat about, Milo sailed toward the shore... Ah, there it was, Bird Island!

The moon rose from out of the dark mainland, flung silver largesse to the waves, invested Bird Island with an aura of milky lambence.

Ahead was the dock, its planks and rails like cigar ash in the moon-light. The wind became less brisk and the water calmed in the lee of the island, and the boat drifted into the dock, a beautiful sleepwalker with its moon-stained sails.

Milo let the boom go, reached for the dock, hauled the boat close. Almost sober, he clambered ashore, shook his fist at the ocean, and prepared to climb the hill.

There was a slight sound behind him.

He wheeled. A dark figure was watching him. Milo's heart caught in his throat. For a long five seconds he stood frozen. At last he mustered his courage.

"Who is it?"

The figure stirred. "Go on home, before you get hurt."

Milo stumbled forward. "Who is it?" The figure slipped off to the side, stooped, arose, struck Milo over the head with a dead branch.

Muttering, Milo fell back, then charged at an object which proved to be a holly bush.

His opponent had disappeared. Nursing his scratches, barks and bruises, he toiled up the ridge to his house.

CHAPTER XII

MILO AWOKE TOSSING and trembling in his bed, shaking off the effects of a bad dream. He hauled himself out of bed, tottered to the kitchen, where he treated himself with Worcestershire sauce, tomato juice, aspirin, Bromo-Seltzer, quinine, hot buttered rum, and orange juice.

He returned to bed and the events of the preceding night began to return to him. With indignation he explored the tender area of his scalp. He flung back the covers, dressed himself, drank a cup of black coffee, set off down the hill.

The air was limpid and cool, the sunlight fell on his shoulders like the arm of a friend, and Milo's hang-over began to ease. He visited the dock, the scene of the crime, and cast about for clues.

But there was nothing to indicate the criminal's identity. And yet — there had been a disturbing familiarity to the lurker. A trick of gait? A tone of voice? … But the longer he thought, the less definite became his impressions. Had it been a man's voice, even? Soft, husky, so he remembered it — but a woman might easily have produced the effect, speaking on a low pitch.

He walked up the path to Miss Pickett's academy. It showed him a blank front, but — like all institutions of learning — a near-silent hum, a confused telepathic ferment, told of intense activity within. Milo hesitated. Everyone would be busy.

He continued along the shore, climbed the hill that hid Mortimer Archer's neat white house from the academy, approached the house.

He pressed the doorbell. The peephole opened, and Archer's liquid brown eye appeared. Milo stared.

The eye vanished. Archer swung the door open.

"Come in, Mr. Green."

Archer had the most spectacular black eye of Milo's experience. He followed Archer into the tidy living room.

"Sit down," said Archer, warmly courteous.

"Thank you." Milo groped for a chair.

Archer belted the scarlet robe tighter around his spare figure. "Could I offer you a bottle of beer?"

Milo shuddered. "Thank you, no. What on earth happened to your eye?"

"It's an outrage," said Archer indignantly. "I heard someone prowling outside last night. When I went to investigate, whoever it was struck me in the eye. When I picked myself up, he was gone."

Milo leaned forward. "Did you recognize him?"

"No," said Archer. "I wish I could. I'd have the rascal arrested."

Milo's nostrils twitched. "You've no idea who it was?"

"None at all. Although," he added thoughtfully, "I might be able to recognize the party if I saw him again."

"Was he big or little?"

"Oh, medium, shall we say?"

"Fat?"

"Not very."

"And you didn't see his face or his clothes?"

"No."

"Then," inquired Milo, "how would you recognize him?"

Archer gave Milo a meaningful look. He left the room, returned with a bottle.

"Smell it," he said.

Milo did so. It was labeled *L'Odorant Prince*, and was pungent with an odor like mingled licorice and orange blossoms.

"I recognized the smell," said Archer. "The next time I smell that on a man, I'll have some questions to ask him."

Milo was not entirely satisfied. He tried to remember the technique of cross-questioning from his reading of murder mysteries, but none of the methods seemed practical in this case. He sighed, sank back in his chair.

"I was attacked also. Last night, about two-thirty or three, on my dock."

It was Archer's turn to be impressed. "Is that so? Not really! What happened?"

"Man hit me with a stick," said Milo shortly.

"And did you recognize him at all?"

Milo frowned. "Yes and no. That is, there was something about him, but I can't quite place it."

Archer gave his bathrobe a twitch, leaned back, offered Milo a cigarette, which Milo refused.

"I mean to get to the bottom of this," said Archer, "although probably it was some tramp from ashore, or maybe a lad visiting someone at the academy. Your boat was not disturbed?"

"No," said Milo, "it wasn't." This aspect of the matter had not occurred to him before. He realized that even though Miss Pickett was extremely rigorous, discreet assignations took place, with unlimited manpower supplied by the nearby universities. The harder it was, the more fun it was.

"Well," said Milo reluctantly, "it's possible, I suppose."

Archer puffed at his cigarette. "How are you doing with your poetry?"

Milo shrugged. "As well as could be expected. The long narrative poem I'm working on should bring in quite a bit. Meanwhile — I'm just knocking out short verses."

"So? And — if it's not too personal a matter — what do they make you?"

"Oh, two-fifty, three-fifty," Milo replied indifferently.

Archer sat up in his chair. "That so? My, that seems quite a good deal. I had no idea a poet could earn so much."

"You have to become established," said Milo.

"How many of these verses do you — er, turn out a week?"

"Oh, when I'm not working on the longer ballad, and not disturbed — perhaps two, three, four a day."

"And you sell all of them?"

Milo said he did. "But I'm not depending on these short ones especially. I'm much more concerned with the success of my longer work... Well, thank you for your help — that idea about the *L'Odorant Prince* especially." He rose and took his leave.

Archer stood looking after him.

"Just goes to show," he muttered to himself, "you never can tell." He shook his head. "Good Lord! Two-fifty, three-fifty a poem! Two, three, four a day! If he ever took a notion to go to work, he could pay for his place in a week."

Milo strode up the tiled walk of the Ottenbright beach house and rang the bell. The door was opened by a blonde young woman in a striking dress of phosphorescent green, vermilion, firefly blue. Milo blinked.

"Good morning," he said. "I was looking for Mr. or Mrs. Otten-bright."

"Jimmy," called the blonde, "man here to see you."

From within came a hushed sound of protest, then Mr. Ottenbright appeared looking round and rosy in a yellow bathrobe.

"Oh, it's Mr. Green...glad to see you. We just got here. Mildred, this is Mr. Green from up on the hill. My stenographer, Mr. Green. We — ah, that is — there are a couple of very important briefs I have to get out and I came over here to work undisturbed." Mr. Ottenbright's slightly protuberant eyes rested on Milo's face uneasily.

"You say you just arrived?"

"Why, yes," said Mr. Ottenbright belligerently. "Don't you believe me?"

"Certainly, of course I do." And Milo explained the nature of his visit.

Mr. Ottenbright licked his lips. "No, Mr. Green, we — that is, I didn't see anyone. As I said, we didn't arrive till this morning."

Thanking Mr. Ottenbright for his help and nodding to the blonde, Milo departed.

He found Ike tinkering with the motor in his launch, the sleeves of his underwear turned gingerly back over his wrists. Beyond Ike and the launch spread the surface of the lagoon, hummocked and swirled by the lazing, black-glinting whales.

Milo's footsteps aroused Ike. He sprang erect, leveled his shotgun, glared a long instant along the barrel; then he lowered the weapon and gave Milo a wave of the hand.

"Hi there," he called. "Glad to see you. I'll tell the ol' woman to put another plate on the table for lunch."

"No," said Milo. "Thank you very much. I really stepped over for some — well, information."

"Information?" Ike was puzzled. "I don't know much for certain. I know lots about whales. Look at 'em out there."

Together they surveyed the cove.

"I went out, caught me six more last week. The buyer's comin' down in a few days, and I wouldn't be surprised…Well, no use blowin' my horn yet, I guess. But there's a nice mess of whale, all full-grown and fat, too, except for a couple of calves — and that pore ol' critter driftin' around by hisself."

Ike's wife came to the door of the shack. "Yoo-hoo," she sang. "Irkham, dear, luncheon will be ready in ten minutes. Wash your hands now."

Ike snorted. "You hear that? Wants me to wash and polish and shine, clean my nails — why I 'spect the woman would tog me out like a dude if I'd give her half a chance! Me, I don't pay no attention to her."

Milo looked at him closely. "That's a new suit of underwear, isn't it?"

Ike glared at him.

"Well — yes. She got me out o' my good ol' flannels that had lots o' wear in 'em yet. I tell you, son, once a woman starts takin' over, a man's got no more chance than a — Well , I shouldn't talk her down, I reckon. She's a good cook, and smart with the dogs. I just wisht she'd get rid o' them high-falutin' notions."

"Yoo-hoo," called the former Mrs. Sipe musically. "Did you hear me, Irkham, dear?"

"Yes, I hear you!" barked Ike. "I'm a-comin' pretty soon." He turned to Milo. "Now what was it you was wantin' to know?"

"It's like this," said Milo. "Last night someone hit me over the head, and I'm trying to get to the bottom of it."

Ike scratched his chin, and his oily fingers left mottled streaks in his whiskers. "You think I done it, son?"

Milo looked out across the cove. "No, not exactly. The truth is, I'm suspicious of anyone and everyone."

Ike shifted the quid in his cheek, spat to leeward through a gap in his whiskers. "Yeah. Do you mean you think I whacked you? Or you don't? I can't seem to figger it out."

Milo shook his head. "No. I'm pretty sure you're innocent." He remembered Mortimer Archer's bottle of *L'Odorant Prince*.

Ike looked suspiciously at him. "How come you're so sartin sure? Maybe it was me."

"No." Milo was more positive than ever as the wind took a sudden veer. "But still — were you home last evening?"

"I was not!" snapped Ike. "I was out with ol' Barber here." He patted the stock of his shotgun. "A-scoutin' for the varmint that's been sneakin' around the corral. An' what's more," he added savagely, "I tangled with him."

Milo stood stiffly. "Tangled with him?"

"Yup. I jumped him over yonder at the point. I didn't get a chance for a shot, but I sure plugged him one in the eye before he took off." Ike displayed a gnarled fist. "Yup, sure got him a juicy one." He turned his gaze across the cove. "Next time," he said reflectively, "maybe I'll get a few shot in his hide."

The door to the cabin opened, and Mrs. O'Rourke emerged with a broom. Ike eyed her truculently, then with increasing trepidation. "Now looka here, woman —"

"Get in to your lunch, you worthless old varmint!" cried Mrs. O'Rourke. "I love you to distraction," she raised the broom threateningly, "but I can't be blinded to your imperfections."

Ike broke into an awkward trot toward the house. Mrs. Winslow Denstrie Sipe O'Rourke bowed to Milo. "Good day, Mr. Green. Isn't it lovely out?"

Milo said yes, indeed it was.

Chapter XIII

Milo pushed open the lobby door and glanced around. Coves stood behind the desk listening to a man whom Milo recognized as Fougasse, Coves' chef, and Coves' face wore a harried expression. Milo took a seat.

The life of the hotel flowed past and around him. The bellhop ran here and there with Martinis, highballs, old-fashioneds, an occasional brandy for the Reverend Dowbrett, from time to time a gin pahit for Mr. Craintree Bezemer, the explorer. Passionate words from the direction of the desk reached his ears: "…the ortolans?…blackguards, scoundrels…"

At last Coves appeared to be free, and Milo approached the desk.

"Why, good afternoon, Mr. Green," said Coves.

"Good afternoon," said Milo. He cleared his throat, leaned forward. "Mr. Coves, offhand, have you noticed anything suspicious here at the hotel?"

Coves' mouth sagged. "What's all this, Mr. Green?"

Milo told his story. Coves listened and took the gravest view of the situation. "It's unthinkable, Mr. Green!"

"You," suggested Milo casually, "were in bed last night between twelve and two?"

"Why certainly, Mr. Green. I never left the hotel! You don't think — you certainly wouldn't suspect that —"

A dark precise little man, Mr. Emmett Tharp, came up to the desk, asked for his mail.

"Did you enjoy the movie in Monterey last night, Mr. Coves?" Mr. Tharp asked.

Coves blushed poinsettia-red. "Why, indeed, yes," he stammered. "Entertaining, very entertaining."

Mr. Tharp nodded and departed.

"How strange," blurted Coves to the silent Milo. "I utterly overlooked going ashore last night."

Milo said stonily, "Do you use *L'Odorant Prince* upon your person, Mr. Coves?"

"Indeed not," Coves assured him.

Cecil Lissacutt approached the desk. "Mr. Coves, do you stock any toilet water besides *Eau de Fou* and *Demoralizing*? Seems to me there was some *L'Odorant Prince* in the case the other day."

"Oh, that! *L'Odorant Prince*! I thought you said — I thought…No, Mr. Lissacutt, nothing else."

Milo left the hotel, crossed the saddle which separated Coves' meadow from that of Miss Pickett. He strode up the gravel walk, entered the academy like a man venturing into a haunted cave.

A girl in the somber academy uniform passed him in the hall, looked back curiously over her shoulder.

"Where can I find Miss Marlowe?" inquired Milo.

"She's in the office," said the girl, pointing the door out to him.

"Thank you." Milo crossed the hall, knocked.

"Come in," said a voice. "Oh," said Celia, "Milo." She rose to her feet. "What are you doing here? Aunt Lydia will skin you alive if she catches you."

"Celia," said Milo sternly, "what were you doing at midnight last night?"

"Why," said the nonplussed Celia, "I was in bed."

"Can you prove it?"

"Just what do you mean, Milo Green?"

"I got hit on the head last night, and I'm checking alibis of everyone on the island."

Her mouth fell open. "Do you think I hit you on the head?"

"No, I don't," said Milo. "But I wanted to be systematic."

"Systematic? You're batty as a bedbug." She laughed. "Who have you — investigated so far?"

"Mr. Archer, Mr. Ottenbright, Ike O'Rourke, Coves — and now you and Miss Pickett."

"I suppose everyone has alibis but us?"

"No," said Milo. "No one has. And everybody seems to have seen the man that hit me. He gave Archer a black eye, and Ike O'Rourke gave him a black eye."

"Milo," said Celia, "you're an idiot. You probably jibbed your boat, and the boom hit you."

"I was on the dock."

"What did you go ashore for in the first place? And who were you boozing with?"

"I went ashore to get my mail," said Milo with quiet dignity. "And I merely had a beer or two with a friend."

"Hm. The post office closes at six, you reel home at two A.M. How you must have nursed those two beers."

"The wind died on me," said Milo.

Celia reached out and patted his cheek. "How's the writing coming, Milo?"

"Fairly well."

"Is it the same thing you were telling me about?"

"No," said Milo. "I've decided to publish a monthly magazine —"

Celia stood back, put her hands on her hips. "Oh, Milo, why don't you try something else besides writing? You'll never pay for your house the way you're going about it. There are other ways to make money, you know."

"How?" Milo asked sullenly.

"Well — there's farming."

He snorted. "Where could I farm? There's nothing but hills on my section."

"They grow rice on hills. In Siam and China and the Philippine Islands. I've seen pictures. They build a lot of terraces and then flood the ground and plant rice. Or you could plant ginseng. There's all kinds of money in that."

Milo gaped at her. "Ginseng? What's that?"

"I saw an advertisement just yesterday in a magazine. It says you can make five thousand dollars an acre. I think it's the roots that are valuable. Wait, I'll get you the magazine."

She returned a minute later and thumbed through the magazine till she found the advertisement. It read:

GROW GINSENG ROOT ! ! !

Make $5,000 an Acre Planted with Our Seed ! ! !
This medicinally valuable herb grows anywhere.

WE BUY YOUR CROP ! ! !

↣ One dollar brings you seed for an entire acre. ↢

ACT TODAY ! ! !

The illustration depicted a large man in a straw hat and overalls, a ranch house in the background.

"Here," said Celia, "we'll send for some seed right away." She tore out the advertisement, pasted it on a card, and wrote Milo's address at the bottom.

"I haven't a dollar with me," said Milo.

"I'll lend you a dollar," said Celia, "and we'll send the letter air-mail special delivery. Now you go home and start digging up an acre of ground."

Milo seized her hands. "Celia."

"Yes, Milo?"

"I love you."

"Do you?"

"Yes. Can't we go somewhere more secluded? There's a prickly feeling at my shoulder blades — almost as if your aunt were staring at my neck."

"She is," came a voice over his shoulder. Milo leapt about to face Miss Pickett.

"What is your business here, Mr. Green? You must know you're not welcome."

"Exactly," said Milo coldly. "I merely wish to inquire: Did you hit me with a stick last night? Over the head, a stick about two feet long, fairly hard wood?"

"I did not. Is that all you wish?"

"That's all — except that maybe it's my duty to warn you that someone on this island will do the wildest deed that comes to his mind — apparently from sheer viciousness. He might even set fire to the academy!"

Miss Pickett's jaw dropped. "Have you any proof of this?"

JACK VANCE

"The proof," said Milo, "resides in a scar on my scalp and in Mr. Archer's black eye — both resulting from blows received on Bird Island. You, Miss Pickett, may be next."

She gasped, clutched her neck with a gaunt, long-fingered hand. "Do you actually believe —"

"I do," said Milo. "The man — if it is a man — will stop at nothing."

"But what can we do?" quavered Miss Pickett.

Milo cleared his throat. "I'll look in once in a while, to see if you're all right."

"Oh, Mr. Green, that would be so gracious of you," said Miss Pickett. "I wonder if we should call in the police?"

Milo shrugged. "How would that help? When the constable is at hand, the criminal lies low. When the coast is clear, he's here and there, slugging people, prowling, lurking..."

"Oh, dear!" exclaimed Miss Pickett.

"Well," said Milo, "I'll be running along."

"I'll walk with you a little way," said Celia, slipping from behind the desk.

Miss Pickett stiffened. "Celia."

Celia slunk back behind the desk. "I guess I'd better finish this chart."

Milo took a diffident leave, turning his back on Miss Pickett with reluctance.

The packet of ginseng seed arrived. Milo pawed through the parcel for planting directions, without result. So he strewed the seed in rows down the acre of soil he had turned, tamped the dirt firmly, watered the acre well, and went indoors to wait developments.

$5,000 an acre — did that mean $5,000 per acre per year? If so, thought Milo, it might be wise to plant a few more acres. He wondered why the retailers bothered with selling seed; surely there would be greater profits if they planted the seed themselves?

The doorbell rang. He glanced at his watch — 10:00 P.M.

Two furtive figures stood outside in the dark.

"Yes? What is it?"

The figures came forward, and Milo relaxed when he saw Coves. The other man was Mr. Turk, the house detective at the hotel.

"We're sorry to disturb you, Mr. Green," said Coves, glancing back over his shoulder into the windy darkness. "But Mr. Turk was making his rounds outside the hotel and saw a dark figure. When he approached, the figure fled — Mr. Turk thinks in this direction. We were wondering..." He left the sentence dangling.

"No," said Milo. "I've seen no one. But then I've been in my study all evening." He snapped his fingers. "It must be the same fellow that slugged me. Just a moment, I'll put on a sweater and come with you."

He ran to a cabinet, pulled a dark blue sweater over his head, returned to the two silent figures at the door.

Milo closed the door behind, and the three started down the road, feeling their way through the night — for a high fog held back the starlight. A wind off the ocean blew dampness into their faces, bit their necks and hands. As their eyes became accustomed to the dark, the ridge and central heights loomed solid black on the near-black of the sky. The sea was lost entirely.

Milo led the way down his road as far as he had graded.

"He's probably got away now," Coves muttered hoarsely. "There's no use running around catching our death of cold —"

"Hark!" hissed Mr. Turk. They all heard a rock rattling down the side of the hill, about a hundred feet ahead of them.

"Let's separate," said Milo. "Surround him."

"Right!" said Mr. Turk. "Mr. Coves, you wait here; Mr. Green, you work down to the right; I'll take the left. When I whistle, we close in."

Coves found himself alone.

Solitary in the windy night, black sky above him, black ground below, nothingness to either side. He wished he hadn't come on this expedition; he turned his back into the wind and stood huddled, waiting for sight or sound.

A shrill whistle from below cut the blackness. The figure crouched, scuttled toward Coves.

"Halt!" cried Coves in a reedy voice. The figure halted, seemed to crouch, then scurried back down the hill.

The retreat released a barbaric flood inside Coves, filled him with a heady exaltation. He sprang forward, yelled "Halt!" again, in a far more assured voice.

"Hah!" he heard Mr. Turk bellow. "No you don't! I've got you!"

Coves ignited his cigarette lighter. The three of them bent, and looked upon a pallid youth of seventeen or so, wearing a red sweater with a white S.

"Umph," cried Mr. Turk. "Stanford, eh? What are you doing, sneaking around in the dark?"

"Yes," echoed Coves, "just what *are* you up to, you young scoundrel?"

"I haven't done nothing," protested the youth. "Leave me alone!"

"What's in that bag?" asked Milo suddenly. He stooped, picked up a paper sack. The captive gave a plaintive cry. "Hey, don't! Don't mix 'em up! I've got thirteen varieties; I only need two more —"

"Thirteen varieties of what?" threatened Mr. Turk.

"Bird manure," said the youth abjectly.

"Bird manure! What do you want with thirteen different kinds of bird manure?"

"Fifteen different kinds," said the youth. "Then I get initiated into Tri-Omicron fraternity. Now lemme up, I ain't no criminal."

"Check on that bag, Mr. Green," said Mr. Turk. Milo gingerly fished out a number of smeared cellophane envelopes, read the labels by the flickering glow of the cigarette lighter: 'Sandpiper' 'Sparrow' 'Sea gull' 'Duck' 'Chicken'.

Milo replaced the bags. "You won't find any tern around here," he said. "Perhaps a few finches, a grosbeak or two, but hardly any tern."

"You hear that?" barked Mr. Turk. "Now get off the island!"

Milo rose at six, dressed, made coffee and toast, scrambled two eggs, squeezed a glass of orange juice, sat down at his big table of polished dark wood and ate his breakfast. Then he wandered downhill to his ginseng patch, searched the ground for vigorous young shoots. After a fruitless five minutes he rose, brushed the soil from his knees. He looked up and down the ridge, debating where to plant more of the golden acres. $5,000 an acre! Ten acres meant $50,000! Or if he harvested two crops a year, five acres would yield him the same amount. If three crops, three and a third acres...

After lunch he walked down the hill to the hotel, where he had arranged to receive his mail. There was a letter from the Ginseng Growing and Receiving Company, Box 523B, Steubenville, Ohio. Milo tore it open.

Dear Sir:

Through an unfortunate oversight we neglected to enclose planting instructions with your shipment of ginseng seed. We take this means to repair the omission.

Sincerely,

R. Bingham, Sales Manager.

Milo scanned the accompanying mimeographed sheet.

Sow seeds one-quarter of an inch apart, one-quarter inch deep in a mixture of moist mold, sphagnum moss, and fine Coraland Brand sand (obtainable from us). Let germinate in a hothouse at a constant temperature of eighty-two degrees Fahrenheit, and at a humidity of not more than 70 per cent, to protect the delicate seedlings from *Sporillia Mortephytes* type fungi. Soil must be moist but never wet. When plants are two years old, transplant to shady, well-drained slightly acid soil on a site protected from wind. Spray plants monthly against aphids, chinch-bugs, cutworms and ginseng moths, with Special Ginseng Protective Liquid (obtainable from us). Protect these delicate plants from frost during cold months by using Little Giant Brand Ginseng-type Smudge-pot (now in stock). When plants are eight years old, harvest with the Double-action Ginseng Root-puller (obtainable from us)...

Milo carefully laid the letter in the fireplace and retired to his study, where he spent the afternoon mixing drinks at the bar, setting them on the electric train and sending them around the room to himself.

Chapter XIV

Like a toy balloon at a tank of compressed air, Miss Pickett's tight little world went up in her face.

During the last few weeks Miss Pickett had noticed a peculiar cessation to the complaints of Madeline Cheabrough, the academy's most versatile hell-raiser, and her cronies Skippy Ballard and J. B. Carr. Miss Pickett had been gratified that the girls were at last submitting to discipline, and so perhaps had failed to maintain her usual vigilance.

Then suddenly Mrs. Cheabrough came striding through the door.

"Why Mrs. Cheabrough —" began Miss Pickett.

Her visitor thrust a magazine under Miss Pickett's nose. "Look at that!" Mrs. Cheabrough's voice was graveled with emotion.

Miss Pickett's mouth sagged. She fumbled at the magazine.

"Where's Madeline?" demanded Mrs. Cheabrough. "Bring her here at once!"

Miss Pickett looked dazedly up from the magazine. "Sue," she instructed a nearby student, "find Madeline Cheabrough, please." She went back to *Nude-Art* magazine. It had fallen open to a well-thumbed page. Displayed was an Arcadian scene — a tree, a young woman demurely studying something in the gnarled branches overhead, perhaps a bird's nest. The tree was unmistakably a Monterey cypress, the nature enthusiast was unmistakably Madeline.

"Miss Pickett!" said Mrs. Cheabrough. "How do you explain this terrible thing?"

Miss Pickett's bosom heaved. "I simply can't understand." On sudden thought she thumbed hastily through the other pages. "Oh," she gasped. For here was the arch Miss Skippy Ballard bending provocatively over a clump of wild daisies, and a little further on she found the enticing Miss J. B. Carr, prone on a sand dune, with sunny highlights along her shoulder blades and upturned feet. "My word!" gasped Miss Pickett. "My word!"

Madeline sauntered down the hall. "Why hello, Mother. What on earth brings you here?"

Mrs. Cheabrough thrust the magazine at her. "Madeline — what does this mean?"

Madeline looked. "Hm. So that's how they turned out. Not bad. Little skinny in the ribs, maybe — only that's the style nowadays."

"Do you know who told me about this?" cried Mrs. Cheabrough. "Mrs. Hugh!"

"Ah!" Madeline nodded. "That nasty little Dicky Hugh spotted it, I bet."

"Do you realize that it's all over town? Do you realize that your reputation is ruined?"

"I don't see why it should be," reasoned Madeline. "Somebody's got to pose for these pictures. We made five dollars apiece that day."

"*That* day!" cried Mrs. Cheabrough and Miss Pickett in unison. "Do you mean there've been others?"

"Every Sunday."

Mrs. Cheabrough turned to Miss Pickett and began to speak. During her fourth topic Mrs. Cheabrough broke off suddenly. "I'm exhausted," she said in a broken voice. "Utterly exhausted! Oh Madeline…" She stumbled to a nearby chair.

Miss Pickett stood awkwardly in the middle of the room. Madeline cleared her throat. Miss Pickett whirled and gave her a terrible look.

"Say, Miss P," said Madeline in a low, hurried voice, "I can fix everything up — for a price." She glanced across the room to where her mother sat with brooding head. "If Mother makes a fuss, you're done for — you and the whole academy. The publicity —"

Miss Pickett tightened her mouth.

"Now, for a few concessions," said Madeline, "such as weekly dances, no limit to our spending money, Friday and Saturday nights out, ice cream three times a week, dancing in the hall to records — in other words, a thorough liberalization of policy — I'll take the rap, and talk Mother into letting me stay here. And I know if she doesn't do anything, Mrs. Ballard and Mrs. Carr won't either, because they simply fawn on Mother. Is it a deal?"

"Is there nothing you wouldn't stoop to?"

"You'd better make up your mind," said Madeline. "Here comes Mother."

"Yes," sighed Miss Pickett.

Madeline slipped across the room to where her mother was struggling to her feet.

"Sit still, darling," she said. "There's been a terrible mistake. Miss Pickett's not at all to blame. Let me explain. You see, we girls took those pictures of each other — to help us in figure drawing, modeling of muscles, light and shadows — you know? A book of photographs costs five dollars — so we each saved five dollars. Well, Skippy took the film to be developed and she lost it in Monterey. And somebody probably picked it up, developed it, and used it in this awful way. I guess there's nothing some people won't do."

The next day Miss Pickett called a meeting of the student body.

Miss Pickett's message was short.

"The suggestion has been made that you young ladies might like to manage your own social affairs through various committees and activity chairmen and so forth. If that is the case, you have my permission, provided that any extracurricular engagements do not interfere with your classroom work ... I am sure that you young ladies will use a measure of discretion, and perhaps impose upon yourselves a set of sensible regulations. I have decided to concern myself only with the academic side of your life here, because I feel that you are all mature and sensible enough to look out for yourselves.

"Another thing, I have decided to relax all restrictions upon your spending money. I wish to remind you, however, that ostentation and vulgarity are synonymous, and that over-indulgence in sweets ruins the complexion, the digestion and the figure.

"Now I think Clarissa Landowne will make a good chairman pro tem. I will leave and you may choose your own governing committees."

She stalked from the room, and the girls recovered from their shock in time to rouse her out with a spontaneous cheer.

An hour later the pupils of Miss Pickett's Academy had formed themselves into a self-governing body. There was a President and Secretary-Treasurer and an Executive Committee. There was a Grievance Committee and a Judicial Committee and a Recreation Committee and a Social Board. Resolution followed resolution. One of the first was a decision to hold a First Annual Grand Ball three weeks from the coming Saturday.

Immediately after the assembly broke up, every girl in the academy retired to write a letter of invitation to some especially favored boy friend.

Miss Pickett, when apprised of the developments, clamped her teeth and said nothing.

Chapter XV

A shadow fell across Coves' face as he stood at the desk checking accounts. Looking up, he saw Tiger Joe Connolly.

"'Afternoon, Mr. Coves," said Tiger Joe. He saw Rexie. "Ha, there's the nice pussy! Ch'k, ch'k, ch'k! Howsa kitty?"

Rexie turned his face to the wall.

"Place stays filled up, eh, Mr. Coves?" said Tiger Joe jovially.

"Yes, Mr. Connolly, it certainly does."

"Must make you a mint."

"Business is fair," Coves agreed distantly.

"Glad to hear it. I like to see a place do good. Especially a nice place like this."

Coves nodded and turned back to his accounts.

The next morning at 7:00 A.M., Coves rose, brushed his teeth, combed his hair with a precise touch. Entering the cool lobby, he was surprised to note the robed figure of Mr. Emmett Tharp stalking apparently from the servants' quarters.

Mr. Tharp's dark face wore a frown.

"Mr. Coves, I appreciate the extension of your service — but, so far, it is incomplete. The shoes have not been returned."

"Shoes?" inquired Coves.

"Exactly," snapped Mr. Tharp. "Where are they?"

"Why, Mr. Tharp," stammered Coves, suddenly noting that Mr. Tharp walked barefoot, "where did you leave them?"

"Outside my door, of course — exactly as your sign instructed."

Coves looked from side to side. "What sign?"

Mr. Tharp pointed out a placard on the landing of the second floor. Coves hurried to investigate. The sign was printed in rude black letters.

NOTICE TO GUESTS!

Before retiring, put all shoes and boots outside
door for free cleaning and polish. They will
be returned before morning. Also all slippers,
moccasins, clogs and galoshes for servicing.

The Management

"See?" said Mr. Tharp.

Coves sank down on the top step.

"I know nothing about it."

Coves faced his hostile guests, each of whom wore footgear of the most primitive improvisation, or else went barefoot.

"Mr. Coves," barked Mr. Boyce, "your enjoyment of this incredibly stupid prank by now must be palling upon you. Will you please distribute our shoes at once?"

"If it's a joke, it's pretty silly," rumbled Mr. Craintree Bezemer.

Coves held up his hands. "Gentlemen, please! I assure you that I have no slightest knowledge of where your shoes are! There's some terrible mistake —"

"Mistake be damned!" roared a tall red-faced man. "If you don't know where our shoes are, who does?"

"Hold on now," said Mr. Turk. "It's probably not Mr. Coves' fault at all. Let's get to the bottom of the matter."

Tiger Joe Connolly descended the steps, his large feet shod in comfortable black shoes.

"Hey," exclaimed Mr. Boyce, "you've got your shoes on!"

Tiger Joe nodded.

"How come? Why didn't you put your shoes out?" inquired a voice from the throng.

"Oh, I didn't want to cause Mr. Coves trouble," said Tiger Joe. "I felt there'd be enough to do with all these other people."

Mr. Boyce stamped savagely toward the stairs. "I'm checking out.

And what's more, if anyone mentions Bird Island Hotel to me, I'll certainly have something to say."

"Mr. Boyce!" cried Coves. "Just a moment! I'm sure there's some explanation!"

Mr. Boyce paused. "Give me my shoes and I'll let the explanations go."

The door to the lobby opened and Al Carper entered.

"'Mornin'." He stared at the array of bare feet, sidled to the desk, laid down a packet of mail.

"Where's everybody's shoes?" he asked Coves.

"Gone."

"I guess I know what's become of 'em."

Coves leaned forward, his plump face quivering.

"I seen a whole mess of shoes and slippers and such in the middle of the bay as I was comin' across. I guess they was your shoes."

A sudden concept sprang into being behind Coves' sweat-beaded forehead. "Gentlemen!" he cried. "I think I know the answer!"

"Well?" was Mr. Tharp's sharp inquiry.

"An attempt is being made to ruin me."

The tall red-faced man snorted. Mr. Boyce turned away in disgust.

"Just a minute," bellowed Mr. Turk. "Let Mr. Coves finish."

"Gentlemen," said Coves, "I assure you that this is sabotage."

"Bah!" snorted Craintree Bezemer. "Who'd want to sabotage you? It can't be competitors. There's not another hotel on the island."

"It wouldn't be competitors," said Coves. "It would be gangsters."

Faces still stared uncomprehendingly.

"I suppose an explanation is due you ladies and gentlemen." Coves looked at his register, at Mr. Turk, over his shoulder at Rexie. "This island," said Coves, "formerly was a gangsters' hangout. When they were apprehended, I bought the island at a tax sale. That was some years ago, of course. Now I wouldn't be at all surprised if they wanted to locate here again. There've been a number of unpleasant incidents. Mr. Green was slugged, and we've seen prowlers around. That's all I know. I've laid my cards on the table."

During the recital, expressions changed slowly—from anger to skepticism, to interest, and at last, conviction.

The tall red-faced man lit a cigar. "So you believe, then, that some-body — one of the gang — stole our shoes just to ruin you?"

"I'm sure of it," said Coves.

"A dirty trick!" exploded Cecil Lissacutt.

"Vicious, vicious," said Mrs. Pedro Charmington from the arms of Ottilie, her maid.

"Well, I for one won't let anyone scare me off," said Mr. Boyce bluntly. "I'll stick it out."

"Of course," said Coves listlessly, "I'll replace the shoes."

"Nothing of the kind," said Mr. Boyce. "Mine were well-worn. I'd merely like to get hold of the scoundrel that stole them."

"Gentlemen!" cried Craintree Bezemer. "I've a notion that may suit us all. Here we are, a number of intelligent men and women, with noth-ing but leisure on our hands. We've seen a crime committed. In fact, we've been personally done dirt to. If it happened in the Congo, I'd find the blighter and make him beg for mercy! I suggest then that all of us bend our efforts and track down the guilty man. He must be here among us, because that note was definitely an inside job."

"I'm with you," said Mr. Tharp.

"Sound notion," said Cecil Lissacutt.

"I'll do my best," announced Mrs. Pedro Charmington.

Tiger Joe Connolly appeared dubious. "Probably no clues around. Seems like a lot of trouble to me."

"There are always clues," explained Craintree Bezemer. "There's al-ways some kind of clue."

Tiger Joe straightened his necktie. "Probably just someone's little joke."

Mr. Boyce looked at Tiger Joe's comfortably shod feet, then at his own, mottled red, white and blue as they were from the unaccustomed exposure. "It's easy for you to find humor in the situation."

Tiger Joe tightened his heavy fists, lurched his shoulders forward. He caught the eye of Mr. Turk, who stood leaning against the desk, and his mouth curved into an ingratiating smile.

"Well, yeah, I guess it was a pretty dirty trick."

"Dirty trick!" snapped Mr. Boyce. "An outrage! Not only against Mr. Coves, but against me! Let he who is guilty beware!"

Tiger Joe yanked at his necktie, pushed his hands in his pockets, slouched to one side.

"Today then," said Craintree Bezemer, "we get ourselves new shoes, and then, Mr. Coves, when we return we'll locate the crook that's trying to wreck your business."

"I don't know how to thank you —" Coves became aware of a grim figure standing just inside the lobby door.

Ike O'Rourke took a couple of steps forward, made a gesture with his shotgun.

"Which one o' you is the varmint I'm looking for?" He gazed from face to face. "Come on now! Stand out and take your medicine!"

"Mr. O'Rourke," stammered Coves, "what's the trouble?"

"Why, I'll tell you, Mr. Coves, there's no trouble. I'm just a-goin' to make a angel outa the man what let my whales loose."

Coves stared numbly.

"I trailed him over the hill comin' toward the hotel, and then a stretch o' gravel choked the sign. But I aim to find the varmint somewheres close by."

"You mean all your whales are — gone?"

"Lock, stock, and barrel. They's two hundred miles away now, all except one ol' sick critter what only stayed because he was too tired to swim out the gate."

The guests had formed an interested ring around the two. "Probably the same scoundrel that stole our shoes."

"Figured on getting in a good night's work," said another.

Coves said, "I simply can't believe that someone here at the hotel would do a thing like that, Mr. O'Rourke."

"I trailed him this-a-way," Ike said accusingly.

"He might have gone on past — up over the hill. Perhaps Mr. Green saw him. Perhaps Mr. Green…" Coves fell suddenly silent.

"Mr. Green, eh?" Ike toyed with the thought. "Allus thought he was the sly one." He tugged at his beard. "Notice he ain't doin' no work to speak of. No sir — just lallygags around the house up there foolin' and figgerin'." He tilted his shotgun. "I claim Green is a no-good loafer, and I'm prepared to say he's the man what's makin' all the mischief."

"Sounds logical," said Tiger Joe thoughtfully.

There was a general murmur of agreement. Mr. Boyce sank into a chair, to take the weight off his gouty foot.

"Perhaps we should concentrate our primary effort on this fellow Green. We'll have to go carefully, however."

Ike looked from face to face. "What's all this?"

"Somebody stole our shoes," explained Mr. Tharp. "Probably the same man that released your whales. We intend to bring him to justice."

Ike grinned mirthlessly. "I'll take care of the justice, me an' ol' Barber here." He tapped his shotgun with a significant finger. "All you need to do is just name the man."

Mr. Tharp cleared his throat frostily. "I'm afraid, Mr. O'Rourke, that you misunderstand the functions of civilized discipline. If, as private citizens, we're able to fix upon the guilty person, we naturally are obliged to turn him over to the authorities."

Ike grunted. He said to Coves, "Well, I'll be lookin' in again. Right now I gotta go out and catch some more whale, if they ain't all headed south."

A chime sounded from the dining room.

"Breakfast is being served," said Coves.

The guests at the hotel, once resolved to unmask the criminal, let no grass grow under their feet. Each strove to outdo the other. No effort was too elaborate or painstaking. Every inhabitant was questioned and cross-questioned by Mr. Tharp. Craintree Bezemer documented and analyzed all the facts of the case. Mr. Boyce, rendered immobile by his gout, sat in the lobby by the hour, deep in frowning concentration. Mr. Lissacutt checked the timetables, learned the neap and ebb of the tides, discovered the time required for Al Carper's launch to make the passage from Monterey.

However, when every clue had been pooled, every fragment of information collated, the most striking fact, perhaps, was the insistence with which everyone maintained his innocence, and none of the wiles, stratagems and pitfalls made a dent in anyone's testimony, not even Milo Green's.

The third day after the theft of the shoes and the releasing of the whales was not the most humdrum of the seven.

Life had simplified no whit for Rexie. The mouse-hallucination still roved the hotel. Three times now Rexie had charged the illusion. Three times this repulsive being had mauled and trounced Rexie to a fare-thee-well. And then there were the malicious acts of tried and trusted Coves, who caught him and put alien substances on his sore — acrid ointments and scalding lotions. If they'd only leave him alone! He had only two resources: to roll his sore in the soothing mud of the meadow and to eat cheese in his cellar sanctuary.

The day in question started off well enough. He enjoyed his usual breakfast of milk and liver hash; he took a quiet walk in the meadow; he rubbed his sore in the soothing dirt. Then, returning to the lobby, he jumped up on the desk beside Coves, arranged himself, and began to wash his paws.

Tiger Joe approached. Rexie looked up in apprehension, but Tiger Joe kindly tickled his ribs and scratched his head — so evidently sincere that Rexie felt at last the misunderstanding was resolved, that finally he and Tiger Joe were on the way to a satisfying friendship.

A few moments later Rexie had occasion to cross the terrace. Spying Tiger Joe, he ran forward, tail on high.

"Ah, you nasty black thing!" hissed Tiger Joe. "Git outa here before I wring your neck!" And he hastened Rexie's departure with a smart blow.

Rexie fled under the hotel. For an hour he crouched there, not daring to speculate.

An aroma drifted past his nose. Of course, the cheese! He rose and made haste to the cheesery.

This room and all its appurtenances — shelves, vats, tables, benches, crocks, and presses — Rexie considered his private domain. Never had he been disputed this dim little room; and he had come to think of the cheesery as a personal dispensation, to be used as he saw fit.

Today a large new vat of curd had materialized for his delectation. He approached, put his paws upon the rim of the tub, sampled the new mixture. Finding it of excellent flavor and better-than-average texture, he settled himself to the feast.

Steps sounded behind him. Rexie looked up in displeasure.

It was Fougasse. He paused in the doorway a moment, blinking.

He became aware of Rexie and a strangled sound forced itself past Fougasse's throat. He took a stride forward. "*Hola!* What is this? Filthy thief, I catch you!" He lunged at Rexie.

Rexie sprang. Unluckily the vat of cheese lay in this direction, and the spring conveyed Rexie to its exact center, where he sank completely out of sight.

He surged, thrust his head clear, blowing and shaking his head. A great hand seized him, pulled him from the sticky mess, flung him to the floor. A furious stamping of feet spurred him to flight.

Away — out the dim cheesery, down the corridor! Away! Leave Bird Island Hotel behind! Rexie raced down the meadow, leapt over the rocks, mounted the hillside.

A gray edifice rose before him. Rexie scarcely paused. A window stood invitingly open, and Rexie plunged within, crept under a chair and crouched to catch his breath.

Coves noticed Rexie's absence about eleven-thirty, when Rexie failed to appear for his lunch. He walked behind the hotel, called, but to no avail.

Coves returned to the lobby, his forehead creased.

Mr. Turk approached. "Cheer up, Mr. Coves. You look like you'd lost your last friend."

"It's Rexie," said Coves simply. "I can't find him. I've looked everywhere."

Mr. Turk shrugged. "Well, he's probably just wandered off somewhere. It's a cinch nobody would steal him or hurt him."

Coves clenched his fists. "That's what I'm wondering. Suppose whoever has been making all the mischief thought he could upset things even more? He might — do something to Rexie just to create confusion."

Tiger Joe Connolly slouched up to join them. "What's the matter, Mr. Coves? Something worrying you?"

Coves said listlessly, "Rexie's gone. We're afraid somebody's taken him."

Mr. Turk bit into his cigar. "If that's what's happened, and we find the man responsible — well, it'll just be too bad, that's all."

Tiger Joe scratched his protruding jaw. "Well, now — you know, I wouldn't be surprised."

"What?" demanded Coves.

"Oh — nothing," said Tiger Joe.

"Did you see something?" demanded Mr. Turk.

"Well — I saw that guy Green this morning down here. He was sort of sneakin' away from the hotel, and he had a sack over his shoulder. I thought it was funny, especially when I seen something inside the sack give a kind of a kick."

Mr. Turk squared his shoulders. "That settles it. Now we know. I'll tell Mr. Bezemer and the others. We'll fix the wagon for this guy Green once and for all."

The news spread rapidly. In five minutes the lobby was massed with an angry crowd.

Cecil Lissacutt said, "Y'know, you can admire a sportin' kind of a crook — the man that stands up to you and gives as good as he takes. But a man who would molest an innocent animal doesn't deserve consideration."

"Depraved creature," sniffed Mrs. Charmington.

"Well, friends?" called Craintree Bezemer. "What do you say? Shall we go up and see what he's got to say for himself?"

"Let's go!" roared the red-faced man.

The guests swarmed outside.

Rexie had fallen asleep under the chair, and only the tumult of the crowd marching up the hill aroused him. He yawned, stretched, and now the cheese which had dried on his fur pulled and crackled. Rexie stood up, shook one foot, then another. He essayed a step forward, and the constricting film of dried cheese broke.

He became aware of his surroundings. He glanced to right and left, sniffed, took a few cautious steps. Everything looked unfamiliar.

He heard a door open, and he heard conversation. Rexie stole forward. The door was ajar.

Rexie ran across the room, ducked out the door into the sunlight, continued along the side of the house. Must be time for lunch, thought Rexie, and turned down the slope toward the hotel.

Behind him came the pounding of feet. He darted a startled glance over his shoulder, a glance which showed him a horde of men with contorted faces.

Rexie laid his ears back, then like an arrow from the bow, he launched himself downhill.

Chapter XVI

MILO ROSE, DUG on his road, wrote several poems, basked in the sun. At one o'clock he threw a red and blue tablecloth on his table, set out some dishes, ate his lunch.

A sound. Milo raised his head, listened. "I guess I left the radio on," he muttered. "Sounds like a crowd. Probably some gang-buster program."

There came a thunderous rapping at the door. Milo crossed the room, inched open the door. Confronting him stood a tall man with beady black eyes and a congested face. Behind this man was ranged a crowd, disgust and rage on every face.

"What do you want?" inquired Milo.

"First of all, Green," said the red-faced man, "we want the cat. Then we're going to thrash you within an inch of your life and run you off the island. You're not fit to live among decent people."

"C'mon," ordered Mr. Boyce, "spring the cat. You're only making it worse for yourself."

"But," Milo protested, "I haven't any cat!"

"Ha!" snorted Craintree Bezemer. "We know better than that!"

"Look here!" bellowed Mr. Boyce, limping forward. "For the last time."

"Why should I lie to you?" cried Milo. "I tell you I haven't any cats!"

Something brushed his legs, and looking down he saw a catlike creature, its fur caked with a whitish substance. It darted between his legs and scuttled around the house.

A roar came from the mob. "No cat, eh?" cried the red-faced man. "Why, you scoundrel, what have you done to the poor beast?" He reached forward, grabbed Milo's shirt, dragged him outside.

"I don't know what it's all about!" protested Milo. "There's been a mistake!"

The man turned to the crowd. "Shall we thrash him here, or take him down to the hotel?"

"Here!"

Milo gave his captor a desperate push, tore himself loose and bounded down the hill.

"After him!" cried Cecil Lissacutt, springing forward.

The crowd flung itself in pursuit.

Milo ran desperately back and forth, but found himself hemmed in against the edge of the cliff. He halted, then skirted the brink, trying to cut past Mr. Tharp and the tall red-faced man. But Craintree Bezemer lunged at him and capture seemed inevitable.

Milo threw himself off the cliff.

Milo peered around the side of the rock. It was late in the afternoon, and the hunt apparently had been abandoned.

He eased himself into the water and began to paddle the fifty yards back to Bird Island.

To the left and high on the crag his house perched; to the right, the cliff scaled down to Coves' beach; directly ahead was the spot from which he had jumped. Milo grimaced as he recalled the whirl, the plunge, the rush of mint-green cold water. He had swum to the islet, hauled himself up on a ledge and there had crouched, secure for the moment.

The ledge was the resort of a tribe of sea gulls which had wheeled and squawked discordantly about his head the better part of the afternoon.

Milo paused in his swimming, let himself ride the swells while he searched for a place to climb ashore. The cliff presented a hostile face, rising sheer from its barnacle-encrusted base. Perhaps he would be forced to swim around to his dock...No — there was a broken place, a little to the right. Holding his head as high as possible, he watched the clear green water rising and falling against the gray rock. On a rough day it would be smashing, surging, flaying, bellowing...Look there, that was odd — that dark spot on the cliff. A cave? Milo trod water, gazed intently. So it was, a narrow opening into Bird Island.

Milo paddled closer, wondering why he had never noticed this odd hole, for he had sailed past in his boat many times. A glance over his shoulder gave him the answer. The big rock where he had taken refuge hid the opening, unless by chance someone wandered between the rock and the cliff.

Interesting, thought Milo. But the water was ice-cold and his most urgent interests were a hot shower, pajamas, a bathrobe, a highball. He swam along the shore and presently was able to scramble up the cliff.

Shuddering and shaking in his clammy clothes, Milo trudged up the crag and home.

Rexie limped into the lobby, jumped up on the desk and, with a weary sigh, laid himself across the register.

"Rexie!" cried Coves. "Where have you been?" He felt of Rexie's fur. "What on earth…"

Fougasse crossed the lobby. He spied Rexie. "Ah, *tiens*," he said vindictively. "That cat will discover a disagreeable event, M. Coves, if I find him again among the cheese."

Coves stared blankly from Fougasse to Rexie, and now the aroma from Rexie's fur reached his nostrils. "Why—he appears to have cheese all over him."

"Exactly," was Fougasse's dry comment. "At ten o'clock I go to inspect the new curding. *Voilà*, the cat, eating like a lord. In his guilt he jumps into the vat. I, Fougasse, extricate him. But he has no shame, that one. See how he has neglected to wash off the evidence of his misdeed!"

Coves said, "Well, you'll have to lock the door—"

"He creeps under the floor," said Fougasse, eyes fixed on the tired and cheese-encrusted Rexie.

Mr. Turk was nearby. He came forward squinting. "Mr. Fougasse, you say you found the cat in the cheese at ten o'clock?"

"Precisely."

Mr. Turk rubbed his chin. "What happened to him then?"

"He ran up the hill."

Mr. Turk turned to Coves, shaking his head dolefully. "I guess whatever Green was carrying in the sack this morning, it wasn't Rexie."

"Probably abalone," said Coves weakly.

"We've done him an injustice," said Mr. Turk.

Coves slumped into a chair. "How in the world can I explain? He could bring action against all of us. Take every cent."

Mr. Turk hitched up his trousers, cocked his cigar to an aggressive angle. "I'll go up and see if I can make him see reason. Perhaps if you made some sort of gesture, gave him a testimonial dinner of some kind, that might soothe him."

"Good idea," said Coves. "I'll tell Fougasse. Good idea, Mr. Turk."

An hour later Mr. Turk returned with a cheerful step.

"Well?" Coves asked anxiously. "Is he coming?"

Mr. Turk shook his head. "Nope. But Green's okay. I apologized for all of us and he said not to worry about it."

Coves rubbed his hands together doubtfully. "Why won't he come for dinner?"

"Well — he says he's got to meet a bus in Monterey. There's a fellow who's coming to spend a week or two with him."

Milo had been pressing his old friend Mahmoud Singh, a mystic and student of the occult, to visit him, and Mahmoud had at last acquiesced.

Milo met him at the bus depot, where his friend's yellow turban set him apart. Milo greeted him warmly, then led him to the dock where his boat was moored.

Mahmoud Singh gingerly settled himself amidships. He was a man of middle height with the silhouette of a cucumber. He had a moon-like face and large eyes of cinnamon-brown. He moved with a studied grace.

The day, though sunny, was somewhat gusty, and the waves of the channel rolled past with crests of white spume. The sailboat behaved accordingly, and Mahmoud Singh grasped the gunwales with both hands.

Milo indicated the house atop the crag, and Mahmoud Singh relaxed his grip long enough to perform a gesture of airy approval.

"I hope you prosper with your writing?"

Milo scowled. "As a matter of fact — no."

"A pity."

Milo swung the bow of the boat into the dock, and the sail rattled down the mast. "I'm not too much of a businessman," he said. "I'm two months behind on the bank payments." He leapt to the dock, holding the boat close in. Mahmoud Singh scrambled heavily up on the rough planking.

"You should seek other sources of revenue," he said, settling his turban on his head.

"There's supposed to be a treasure hid on the island," said Milo. "I've looked high and low, and I guess everybody else has, too."

"Perhaps your methods were at fault," suggested Mahmoud Singh, stamping first one foot, then the other, to adjust the drape of his blue serge suit.

"How do you mean 'at fault'?"

"Did you send out Questing Vibrations?"

Milo admitted that he had not resorted to this measure.

"Of course you put yourself into a supra-somatic state?"

Again, Milo had to confess his neglect.

Mahmoud Singh sniffed. "The first things which should occur to one."

Milo eyed his guest with a trace of acrimony. "Perhaps tomorrow, or the next day, you'll see if you can locate it yourself."

"As you wish," said Mahmoud Singh impassively. "Though it may be…"

"What?"

"It is nothing," said Mahmoud Singh.

Luckily Mahmoud Singh's luggage was light, consisting only of a few spare turbans, assorted incenses, hair oil, a toothbrush. At last they reached the top of the crag and Milo ushered Mahmoud Singh into his home.

Mahmoud Singh professed himself delighted with all, especially approving the stairway to the study, displaying as it did the Vedantic deities.

Dinner was served, and shortly afterwards Mahmoud Singh announced that he had too long neglected a spiritual discipline which he called 'going into the silence'. Stating that he would be occupied all night with his concentrations, he arose.

"You look tired," said Milo anxiously. "Perhaps you'd better get some sleep instead."

"Sleep?" scoffed the mystic. "Pah! I have no time for anodyne. Sleep must remain a rare thing for me until I have mastered the *tattva*."

"*Tattva?*"

Mahmoud Singh smilingly raised his dark eyebrows.

"The followers of the Sankhya and Yoga schools recognize twenty-five principles — the *tattva* — though the Yoga has added a theistic twenty-sixth: that is, the *Nirguna Purusha*, or the self devoid of qualities. You follow me?"

In the main, Milo said, he did.

Thereupon Mahmoud Singh said good night.

The following morning Milo, peering into Mahmoud Singh's room, found the ascetic still deep in his self-imposed trance. Luckily Mahmoud Singh had fallen upon the bed rather than upon the hard floor, and in some manner had thrust himself under the bedclothes.

Milo tapped Mahmoud Singh's plump shoulder, and Mahmoud Singh returned to reality with a sigh.

"Good morning," said Milo. "Like some breakfast?"

"Ah — um," said Mahmoud Singh, rolling up on his elbow and fixing Milo with blank eyes. "Breakfast. Yes. Excuse me, I will compose my dress. Ah, today," he mused, "the sign of the lizard. The aquamarine turban it shall be."

Milo returned to the dining room, and presently Mahmoud Singh made his appearance.

After breakfast as Mahmoud Singh sipped his coffee, especially brewed in a small copper brazier fired by camel dung, Milo leaned forward impulsively.

"I've been thinking over your offer," he said.

Mahmoud Singh raised a polite eyebrow.

"About the treasure," explained Milo. "You said you might be able to send out some kind of astral spirit."

"Ah, so I did." Mahmoud Singh passed a hand gracefully across his forehead. "True. And yet, strange to think, what treasure can be fuller, richer, more complete than tranquillity of the spirit? I advise you, my friend, to seek rather for peace and the experience of the Higher Planes."

Milo made an impatient gesture. "Peace and tranquillity? When I'm either being hit over the head or hunted and harried across the island like a fox? No, the most practical avenue to peace and tranquillity is to find the treasure and then retire."

"Perhaps the treasure is burdened with a curse," suggested Mahmoud Singh. "In this case, I would be rendering a disservice." He shut his eyes and relaxed even more completely into the chair.

"That's a risk I'll have to take," declared Milo recklessly.

Mahmoud Singh sighed. "So…Just so. This afternoon, perhaps. Yes, this afternoon I shall project a questing vibration through the island. If the treasure exists, it shall be found."

"Wonderful!" exclaimed Milo. "Though really, so far as I'm concerned —" He looked at his watch, but meeting Mahmoud Singh's limpid glance of inquiry, shrugged. "If you'd like, I'll show you my ginseng patch."

"Delighted," said Mahmoud Singh.

As they walked back and forth across the clods, Mahmoud Singh discussed ginseng root in all its aspects, though he himself attributed few extensive or peculiar powers to the substance.

"It is true however," he added, "that certain Nepalese tribes prepare an infusion of ginseng in tiger urine for use as a specific against chest congestion, reportedly to good result."

They returned inside, and Mahmoud Singh at once retired to his room to prepare himself for the exercise of the afternoon. He failed to appear for lunch, and not until two-thirty, when Milo knocked on his door, did the ascetic manifest himself.

"Are you ready?" called Milo. "I've got a shovel and a pick, also a hatchet, in case we run into any roots."

"Umph," groaned Mahmoud Singh. "If this be the will of the Eternal, I must submit."

Presently he joined Milo in the living room.

"Is there anything you need?" Milo asked.

"No," said Mahmoud Singh. "I will merely require a seat, adequately comfortable, where I may compose the corporeal frame while the Seeking Essences wing and soar about the island."

Milo frowned thoughtfully. "Won't the Seeking Essences be hard for me to follow?"

"We will all go together," decided Mahmoud Singh.

He seated himself, closed his eyes, and began to mumble phrases whose gist Milo could not catch. The mutter died to a mumble, to stertorous breathing, while Milo hovered close.

Mahmoud Singh's plump hands began to tremble, to twitch. They grasped the arms of the chair, and his arms were stiff and rigid. His eyes snapped open, passed across Milo with no recognition. He heaved erect, and suddenly strode from the house.

Milo shouldered his tools, but after fifty yards Mahmoud Singh stopped short, frozen in his tracks. Milo waited uncertainly nearby.

Mahmoud Singh shuddered and swayed, as if pulled by rival forces. At last he turned, stalked stiffly down the hill in the direction of the hotel, over the rocks, across fallen logs, past thickets, through the grove of cypress trees at the foot of the hill. And Milo, ever more dubious as the hotel bulked larger ahead, hurried in his wake.

"Mr. Green, just a moment!" called a resonant voice. It was the Reverend Dowbrett, jauntily waving a long alder switch.

Milo made a gesture signifying silence. The puzzled cleric, increasing his stride, fell into step beside Milo.

"Who's that?" He motioned to the hurrying figure in the aquamarine turban.

"A friend of mine," Milo explained in an undertone. "He's in a hypnotic trance — looking for the treasure."

The Reverend Dowbrett stared even more attentively after Mahmoud Singh.

"That's astounding, isn't it? Does he actually believe he can find it?"

Milo nodded. "Mahmoud Singh's a student of the occult."

The Reverend Dowbrett looked quizzically at Milo. "Surely you, a sound Christian, don't hold to that heathen rubbish?"

Milo shrugged. "If he finds the treasure, I won't be critical of his methods."

"Paganism," scoffed the Reverend Dowbrett.

"I wonder," muttered Milo, "if Mahmoud Singh is heading for the hotel... Looks as if he is. But why?"

The entranced mystic indeed appeared bent on the hotel. He rounded the corner of the building, stepped up on the terrace, turned into the lobby. Accelerating his pace, he made for the bar, thrusting aside the startled Mr. Turk, just emerging.

"Ha, what's this?" bawled the house detective. Mahmoud Singh stopped short, shuddered, and put a hand to his eyes.

Milo advanced swiftly. "Are you all right? You don't feel faint?"

"Where am I?" muttered Mahmoud Singh.

"I'll get you some brandy."

Mahmoud Singh gratefully tossed off the restorative, and became something more like his usual self.

Milo was eager to learn what, if anything, had been the message of the Seeking Essences, but Mahmoud Singh declared himself puzzled. "I cannot fathom," he tapped his chin with a speculative forefinger, "the reason for my being conducted here." He passed his hand across his eyes.

"Are you sure you're all right?" inquired Milo. "Would you like more brandy?" Milo started for the bar, hesitated, looked back to the Reverend Dowbrett. "It's a little early in the day yet, but perhaps you'd join me in a brandy yourself, Reverend?"

The Reverend Dowbrett glanced at his shoes, teetered on his heels. "Well, as you say, it is rather early in the afternoon — but I must confess that I've a weakness for good brandy."

After a third brandy, which the Reverend Dowbrett insisted on administering, Mahmoud Singh declared himself fully recovered.

"Perhaps then you'll be able to resume the trance?" asked Milo.

Mahmoud Singh, after a moment's hesitation, admitted that the Seeking Essences might not be entirely depleted.

"Umph," snorted Mr. Turk. "I wish I had a dollar for every swami I pinched when I was on the force in Los Angeles."

Mahmoud Singh placed himself in a comfortable chair, adjusted his turban, closed his eyes, spoke a few rapid phrases.

Milo, the Reverend Dowbrett, and Mr. Turk watched the recumbent form breathlessly. Mahmoud Singh gave a guttural cry, sprang erect, moved swiftly for the door, and Rexie, in the center of the lobby, had to leap nimbly aside to avoid the portly mystic's tread.

Mahmoud Singh now pursued an erratic course. He started up the side of the hill where the slope was steepest, the thicket the most dense, the sunlight the hottest, and the Reverend Dowbrett was soon gasping and perspiring. Then, just as Mahmoud Singh seemed intent on clawing his way up a perpendicular shoulder of sandstone, he changed direction and bent himself along the side of the hill toward the sea.

"Looks like Mahmoud Singh is returning to the house," Milo said to the panting but game Reverend Dowbrett. "It's almost in this direction."

"I'm sure I can't predict his plans," gasped the Reverend Dowbrett. "I wouldn't be surprised if he jumped into the ocean and began to swim for Cocos Island."

But Mahmoud Singh stopped about fifty feet short of the brink of the cliff, just below Milo's house, planted his feet firmly on the stony ground and gazed fixedly at the toes of his pointed yellow shoes.

"But that's all rock!" gasped Milo. "You couldn't bury a phonograph needle there, let alone a treasure. However..." He looked over his shoulder, then out to the islet where he had taken refuge from the amateur detectives. It rose from the water almost opposite to where Mahmoud Singh had placed himself.

In sudden excitement, he scrambled across the rocks to where Mahmoud Singh stood intently eyeing his yellow shoes.

Milo ran to the edge of the cliff. "Right here is where I jumped off, and down there..." He whirled and ran up the hill.

"Mr. Green!" called the Reverend Dowbrett, hastening after him. "Where are you going?"

But Milo only ran the faster, and the Reverend Dowbrett gave his own short legs an added exertion. Mahmoud Singh, fixed in position, maintained his vigil.

The Reverend Dowbrett joined Milo just as Milo was pushing off in his boat.

"Where," panted the cleric, "are we going?"

"I may be wrong," said Milo, "but I think I know where the treasure is."

The Reverend Dowbrett sat silently in the stern while Milo hoisted the sail and steered around the island.

To their right rose the rock; above and to the left Mahmoud Singh stood silhouetted on the sky above the cliff. Directly ahead a sharp black line showed, which, as Milo rounded a protecting shoulder of rock, became an opening into the inner parts of the island.

Three minutes later Milo had unshipped his mast, laid it in an untidy clutter of spars, sails and rigging along the deck. He dug the paddle into the water. The boat sped for the narrow opening. "Duck!" called Milo. For a moment all was dark; then their eyes became accustomed to the dimness. To the right rose a shining barnacled wall; ahead sloped a meager beach of white sand; to the left stood another wall with a rough ledge running ten feet above. On this ledge rested a great number of decayed wooden crates, through which glinted a dark and vitrine substance.

Milo craned his neck. "Can that be the treasure?"

They jumped to the beach, scrambled up to the ledge. With excited hands Milo tore open a crate, drew forth a bottle, peered at the label. The Reverend Dowbrett laughed an exultant laugh.

"Treasure! Ha, Mr. Green — more than treasure! Three-Star Hennessy." He indicated each of the significant marks. "Bottled," he peered at the label, "in 1882. Ha, Mr. Green, each of these flasks is a treasure in itself."

CHAPTER XVII

AT MISS PICKETT'S, light glowed from every window, streamed out the door. The auditorium was like the pavilion of a caliph's bhang-dream, with its many-colored shadows, swooping tapes, shining floor. The air held a fragrance. Miss Pickett supervised the arrangement of the buffet. And everywhere were girls in their gowns of rose, dark blue and magenta, orange, black and white, chartreuse, nut-brown, tangerine, red, saffron, maroon, sea-green. Everywhere were girls — girls with their hair up, girls with their hair down; bold girls and shy girls; girls smooth as long grass and girls gay as buttercups; girls, girls, girls.

Guests were trickling slowly into the hall, parking their topcoats; and on the bandstand Scurvy Murdock was arranging the disposition of his Twentieth-Century Troubadours.

Celia wore a gown of crinkly dark brown, full in the skirt with gold tape at the waist, and gold slippers peeped and glinted under the hem as she walked. Her hair had been brushed till it glowed rich and deep as the lights in sunlit ale. Her eyes were bright with excitement.

Miss Pickett drew near, eyed Celia like a butcher estimating a side of beef.

"Celia, isn't that gown a trifle extreme?" She sidled around to inspect Celia's silhouette — herself wearing an ankle-length garment the color of wet sidewalk. "It seems to me you could loosen your belt a trifle; it makes your — your hips so prominent."

Celia turned away from the inspection. Miss Pickett looked across the room. "I hope none of those young men have brought liquor. Well, I suppose it's the way the world is going. I wonder if Mr. Coves will come tonight?"

Celia twisted her head. "Mr. Coves?"

Miss Pickett said frigidly, "I thought it might add to the tone of the occasion if Mr. Coves brought some of his guests. He has some very distinguished people staying at the hotel."

Celia had nothing to say. And now as Scurvy Murdock gave his band the beat for *Splashrack*, his theme, Miss Pickett strode away.

Celia waited uncertainly by the door. Where was Milo? He had promised to come early and help her take care of the buffet. A group of people entered the room.

"Why, good evening, Mr. Coves," cried Celia. "Aunt Lydia said you might drop over."

"Yes," said Coves, with an odd glance to the man at his left — a short gentleman in clerical garb. "Miss Marlowe, the Reverend Dowbrett."

"Delighted," said the Reverend, eyeing Celia with approval. Celia looked closely at her new acquaintance, darted a sudden glance of wild surmise at Coves. Coves nodded slightly in embarrassed deprecation. It was plain to see that the eminent free-thinker reveled in a state of advanced exhilaration.

Celia became aware of another figure behind Coves, a hulking, heavy-shouldered man with a jaw like the toe of a logging boot.

"Excuse me," said Coves, noting the direction of Celia's glance. "Miss Marlowe, Mr. Connolly, another of my guests."

The Reverend Dowbrett was peering through the doorway into the ballroom, where the dancers swirled to Scurvy Murdock's urgent reed section.

"Delightful," said the Reverend Dowbrett. "Miss Marlowe, would you honor me by dancing?"

Celia hesitantly let herself be clasped to the rotund form. Then they were away in a whirl, the Reverend Dowbrett agilely performing a step unlike anyone else on the floor, a hybrid of schottische and cakewalk.

"Ah, Miss Pickett," said Coves, "good evening."

"Mr. Coves, I'm so glad you could come. Are you alone?"

"No, Reverend Dowbrett and Mr. Connolly came with me. The Reverend Dowbrett is dancing with your niece and Mr. Connolly...Hm, he was right here a moment ago. There he is, by the punch bowl. I can only stay a moment, but I wanted to see the academy in its party clothes, so to speak."

Tiger Joe, after a furtive look to left and right, poured into the punch bowl the contents of a little bottle he took from his pocket — a thick murky fluid.

Then he sidled up to the wall and waited with an expression of bland expectation.

The Grand Ball proceeded; murmur, laughter, shuffle of feet, rich dimness cast by the carnival lights — all invested the hall with an unreal, dreamed effect. The girls shimmered past in the arms of their escorts.

Intermission. Celia moved a step back from the puffing clergyman, and her face in the dimness was a pale triangle with dark shadows for eyes. She looked toward the door. Coves had taken his leave; her aunt had stepped out of the room. Where was Milo?

The lights brightened to a soft pink-and-amber suffusion. The couples moved toward the buffet laughing and talking, their eyes — even as those of Tiger Joe Connolly — fixed on the frosted punch bowl.

"Milo!" cried Celia, running to meet him. "You're finally here... But Milo!" in quick alarm. "Your clothes! Where have you been?"

"Darling," said Milo, "I've found the treasure."

"Milo! Not really!"

"I certainly have. We'll be married right away. I can support you now," he said proudly.

"Oh Milo! But the treasure —"

"Ah, there's the Reverend Dowbrett. He was with me when I found it. Did he tell you anything about it?"

"No," said Celia. "He's high."

Milo nodded. "I know. I took him back to the hotel in my boat."

"Milo — tell me about the treasure."

"Would you like to see it?"

"Of course! Oh Milo, I'm so thrilled!"

"Let's go," said Milo, "while your aunt's not looking."

They slipped out the doors into the darkness, and off along the leafy trails of Bird Island.

A peculiar phenomenon was occurring near the punch bowl. As each couple sipped their punch, their gay talk would gradually die to hesitant murmurs; they would stare at each other, startled understanding in their eyes; they would clasp hands, oblivious to all but themselves.

Miss Pickett had left the hall.

"How I love you!" Clarence Allen told his date, Madeline Cheabrough. "And I never realized it until just this instant."

"It's strange," sighed Madeline, pushing her silky blonde hair back. "I love you too. It hit me all at once."

"Darling," breathed Clarence, "I want you to marry me."

"Any time, any time at all," agreed the shameless Madeline. "Oh Skippy!" she called to a nearby crony. "Congratulate us! Clarence and I are going to be married!"

"Why, Madeline, isn't it wonderful? Paul and I are too!"

"Same here!" chorused several others.

The Reverend Dowbrett moved slowly forward. "Marriage is a blessed state," he declared. "Finest thing in the world. You all have my heartfelt congratulations."

"Thank you, Reverend," said Madeline, "and perhaps you'll actually be the one to marry us!"

"Of course I will," said the cleric. He fumbled in his pockets. "I haven't got a Bible here, but I know the routine pretty well. Step over here."

"Now?" gasped Madeline.

"Sure," said Clarence.

"We'll be married too," said Paul.

"So will we."

"And we."

"And we."

"And us," said a member of the Stanford varsity football team.

"Everybody got rings?"

There was a fumbling and search — rings of every sort were pressed into service, until at last every couple was provided for.

"Everybody ready?" called the Reverend Dowbrett, supporting himself on the snare drum.

"Go ahead," came the chorus.

" — repeat after me, 'With this ring I thee wed'."

"With this ring I thee wed," came the chorus.

"Put on the ring," commanded the Reverend Dowbrett.

Miss Pickett, prim and tidy, appeared in the doorway.

"I now pronounce you," intoned the Reverend Dowbrett sonorously, "men and wives — with my blessings on all of you."

Miss Pickett's scream cut short the first series of connubial embraces. Startled faces were turned to behold Miss Pickett tottering.

A throng of would-be assistants quickly surrounded her. But the Reverend Dowbrett took command.

"Back!" he bawled. "Stand back everyone! Give her air!" The press loosened. "Here, you, Mr. Connolly, carry her to the bench. Careful now. Get her a drink of water," he tossed over his shoulder to Clarence Allen.

Clarence Allen looked helplessly here and there for a supply of the desired fluid. "Punch should do as well," he muttered. He ran with a glass of punch to the Reverend Dowbrett.

"Ah, Miss Pickett," exclaimed the cleric, "you feel better now? Here, drink a bit of this." And he poured punch between Miss Pickett's pale lips. She swallowed, sighed, swallowed, and then fell into a racking spasm of coughing.

"Easy, easy does it!" cried the Reverend Dowbrett, handing Tiger Joe the glass of punch, while he massaged Miss Pickett's back.

Tiger Joe had been watching attentively. Abstractedly he raised the glass, gulped.

Miss Pickett recovered from her fit of coughing. She reeled uncertainly to her feet. Her eyes met Tiger Joe's.

"Darling," husked Tiger Joe, "I know I'm not good enough to lick your shoes…"

"Silly lad," sighed Miss Pickett. "I've waited so long."

"Honey, you'll marry me?"

Miss Pickett bridled. "Of course, my wonderful Joe."

"Reverend," and Tiger Joe led the coy Miss Pickett forward, "will you go through that little ceremony just once more? We missed out on the last one."

CHAPTER XVIII

MORTIMER ARCHER WAS BUSY at his correspondence when the door jarred to the *thud-thud* of Tiger Joe's knuckles.

Archer admitted his friend, who brushed past into the living room. Archer, wearing his maroon dressing gown, strolled behind. Tiger Joe slumped into the overstuffed chair. Archer lounged against the door.

"Well, sucker?"

Tiger Joe twisted his lip in the beginnings of a snarl, changed his mind, and said instead, "Get us some beer, Slippy."

Archer obliged.

"Well, what's the story?" he asked.

Tiger Joe frowned, bent his face over cupped hands to light a cigarette. "I got married. That's all there is to it."

"On purpose?"

Tiger Joe blew out a long plume of smoke. "Do I look like the kind of guy what don't know which side is up?"

Archer hitched himself into a chair. "Well, what's the deal then? Are we in this show together, or are you throwing in with your — wife?"

Tiger Joe flushed.

Archer made an urbane gesture. "It's none of my affair. I can't see that I've lost anything."

Tiger Joe snorted in vindictive triumph. "I *thought* you hadn't heard! Otherwise you wouldn't be so pleased with yourself."

"Heard what?"

"I thought so. Well, Slippy, you and me have been caught with our britches dragging in the dirt. You remember telling me about some kind of loot Big Ben Manzio had left on the island?"

"What about it?"

"Well, that guy Green got hold of some swami friend of Ben's —
that's the way I figure it — and the swami put him wise to the cache.
Anyway, Green's been hauling old French likker out of a cave by the
boatload."

"No!" Mr. Archer sagged into his chair.

"Hurts, don't it Slippy?"

"I suppose you're tickled silly?"

"I'm married to a paying proposition. I ain't so dumb. I talked the
old lady into startin' an open-air dance hall down near the beach. We'll
clear two, three grand the first night…You ought to see the old lady.
Remember Trampy Scarro the week before he got bumped? The old
lady's the same way, waiting to hear from all the mothers. There's gonna
be some screamin' and yellin'."

"Where are all the brides and grooms? They didn't leave the academy?"

Tiger Joe lifted his lip in a leer. "Hell no. The Reverend sobered up
and told them it wouldn't work. But the old lady's still scared."

Archer watched him with an expression of poorly veiled amuse-
ment. "You mean you're going through with it?"

"Certainly," snapped Tiger Joe. "Don't forget that dance hall. We'll
be cleanin' up. I ain't so dumb, Slippy."

"You're dumb enough in throwing away what the gang made in the
old days. Five grand a week plus!"

Tiger Joe hunched the muscles in his shoulders. "It just happens I
ain't throwin' away no five grand plus."

"How do you mean?"

"I mean we're partners like we always was, and don't forget it."

Archer shrugged. "You can't ride two horses. Who are you going
with — me or old lady Pickett?"

"Neither one," snarled Tiger Joe. "She's coming with us. I'm the
boss. All we got to do now is blast out Coves, Green, Ottenbright and
O'Rourke."

"Green's set, with all that liquor," mused Archer.

"That stuff's like gold, these days."

Archer rubbed his chin. "It all depends on how soon he finds a buyer, and if he sells it all in one piece. He'll get his price, anything he asks, if he waits long enough."

Tiger Joe nodded. "He's settin' pretty good, no denyin' it."

"Well," blurted Archer, "instead of lounging around here drinking beer, why aren't you doing something about it."

"Do something? Why, man, I've been raising particular hell every which way!"

"The only one you really fixed was that old sourdough, when you turned the whales loose."

Tiger Joe glowered through the window.

Archer sat up in his chair. "Well, we've got to stop that guy Green. And I think I know how to do it. Without letting ourselves out in the open at all."

Milo walked down the beach past the hotel toward the dock, where Al Carper's launch was shortly due.

Presently the launch appeared and conveyed him ashore.

Climbing the concrete steps to the street, he noticed a large placard tacked to a telephone pole:

Dance Under the Stars
at
LOVER'S LEAP PAVILION
on romantic

BIRD ISLAND

Featuring the Mesmerizing Music of
SCURVY MURDOCK AND HIS ORCHESTRA
Launches will run at fifteen-minute intervals
from the foot of Alvarado Street.

Milo shook his head, grinned ruefully, walked up into the center of town, entered the lobby of the Val d'Oro Hotel.

"Good morning, Mr. Green," said the potbellied clerk. "Haven't seen you for some time. Great doings out on Bird Island. Wish I'd been to that dance."

"Yes. I suppose it was quite an affair," said Milo. "Has a Mr. Hens-paugh checked in?"

The clerk nodded. "Yes, he's in his room."

"Will you tell him I'm waiting for him?"

"Certainly, sir."

Milo walked restlessly up and down the lobby. A large paunchy man in a sorrel suit approached, smoking a cigar.

"You Milo Green?"

Milo turned his head.

"Oh — hello. You're Mr. Henspaugh, I suppose. Well, if you'll come with me, I'll show you the liquor. I'm in a hurry to close the deal, so I hope you've come prepared. You'll have to haul it away yourself; I haven't any facilities."

"That's all being taken care of," said the big man. "Yep, we've got a crew loading it into the launch right now."

Milo blinked. "That's pretty fast, isn't it? After all, we haven't come to any definite price."

"Price? Hah!" The big man flipped back his coat, to display a nickel-plated star. "I'm McDeever, Board of Equalization. Here's the papers confiscatin' all that contraband likker."

Milo uttered a poignant cry. "Wait! I'm just selling it!"

"Lucky you didn't," said McDeever. "You'd sure land in jail. Don't you know that's a felony, dealin' in smuggled likker?"

"But it's been here for years," argued Milo. "It must be — well, legiti-mate by this time."

McDeever shook his head ponderously. "You'll have to chew that out with them sea-lawyers in Sacramento. I got a call tellin' me about a big cache of likker without them pretty blue stamps. I don't ask how old it is, I just naturally reach out and confiscate it in the name of the law."

"Mr. McDeever," croaked Milo, "have a heart. This sale means ev-erything to me. My whole future depends on it!"

McDeever spat unemotionally. "Durn tootin'. About ten years' worth if you'd accepted money for that there likker."

"I'll pay the taxes!" cried Milo.

"Too late now. That likker's been confiscated. Wasn't yours to begin with. If I was you, I'd just take a quick fade-out and not try to make too much trouble."

Milo turned away. A middle-aged man in a gray sharkskin suit and rimless pince-nez approached with outstretched hand. "Mr. Green? I'm Samuel Henspaugh."

Milo jerked his thumb toward the burly back of Ed McDeever. "There's the man to see. Not me. I haven't a dram to my name."

Twenty feet distant a face peered from behind a newspaper, watched Milo's sagging figure leave the lobby. The paper dropped, Archer rose to his feet, lips pursed complacently. With a contemptuous glance toward Ed McDeever in the phone booth, he strolled out to the street, turned toward the bay.

Along the sea wall he met Ike O'Rourke, who would have passed him by had not Mortimer Archer greeted him expansively, remarking that Mr. O'Rourke seemed uncommonly preoccupied.

Ike paused, searched Archer's face narrowly. "Well, what of it? I'm in a hurry. Dang ol' whale died on me; it's already smellin' up the whole cove."

"My word," said Archer. "What on earth do you do with a dead whale?"

Ike spat to the pavement. "I'll just tow the hulk out to sea, tie a chunk o' rock to it, dynamite the carcass so it don't float. Nothing to it."

A felicitous idea formed behind Archer's distinguished temple. "You know it's hardly an hour ago I was speaking on the telephone to a man in the fertilizer business. I think I could buy that whale from you and make a profit on it."

"Buy it? Humph, take 'er," snorted Ike. "She's yours. Glad to get rid of the dang thing."

"Well," said Archer, "I'll drop by your cabin early tomorrow morning. Incidentally — keep the deal quiet, will you? It's not a very dignified transaction, but I need the money."

"Sure, sure, I'll keep my mouth shut." Ike turned back toward the pier.

About noon the next day, a familiar *putt-putt-putt* reached Ike's ears. Opening the cabin door, he saw his launch, guided by Mortimer Archer, nosing back into the cove.

"Well, you made a quick trip," he said, when Archer finally joined him on the dock. "Lot quicker'n I expected. The boat run okay?"

Archer shook his head dolefully. "It's been a very unfortunate day for me, I'm afraid."

Ike narrowed his eyes. "How come? I thought you had everything planned out."

"I hardly got out to sea," said Archer, "when the rope broke, and I lost the whale."

"You lost the whale?" ejaculated Ike O'Rourke. "How come? Why didn't you tie on again?"

"The whale sank," said Archer.

Ike's jaw dropped. "That's sure strange. Never heard of that before. Usually you can't sink one o' the things for money; now you say this one just up and sank of its own accord?"

"Well, it's gone, and I've had all my trouble for nothing."

Ike muttered under his breath. "There's gonna be some hard words if that whale floats ashore. Maybe we'd better keep quiet about the whole business. No sense askin' for a lot of trouble."

"You're right there. Well, better luck next time."

A few minutes later he took his leave. Ike stared after him, shaking his head. "Dang landlubber. Can't even tow a whale right."

CHAPTER XIX

COVES AWOKE FROM a restless slumber with the sense of something amiss. He heaved himself up on his elbows, consulted the alarm clock. Seven-thirty. He had not overslept. He glanced across the room. Rexie was safe and sound, curled on his pillow.

As Coves watched, Rexie awoke, stretched his legs, yawned widely; then, raising his head with a surprised jerk, he tested the air with his nostrils.

And now Coves comprehended the agency which had aroused him. It was an odor — an odor which, in spite of its low concentration, grasped and suffused and made vile each separate particle of the atmosphere.

Coves hurriedly invested himself with clothes, hastened to the lobby. Here the stench was strong indeed, a ripe, unctuous smell that thickened the air. Mr. Emmett Tharp stood by the entrance, gazing down at the beach.

"Good morning, Mr. Tharp," said Coves, peering from the door. "What in the world is that awful smell?"

"A dead whale has lodged on the beach, Mr. Coves."

Coves kneaded his forehead with his knuckles. "What on earth am I going to do?"

A burly figure descended the stairs. Mr. Turk. "My God, Mr. Coves, there's a chife you could drag around on a hook."

Coves had sagged into a chair. "I'm done for. I might as well close up right now."

A slight breeze fanned their faces; they swayed back as if by the pressure of a hand. It was indeed a titan among smells: a ripe, heady, animal smell; sharp, sweet, sour. It was a scent that suggested scorched sheep intestines, an incredible monumental decay.

Cecil Lissacutt entered the lobby. He spoke in a hushed voice. "Mr. Coves, I've walked the back alleys of Calcutta, I've waded the mud flats of the Yellow River at low tide, I've been downwind from a hyena drowned in the Bombasa sulfur springs...Never, never, Mr. Coves, have I encountered the equal of this magnificent stench."

Mr. Turk stared out at the black hulk on the beach. "I suppose it's more of the dirty work that's been going on."

Coves lurched to his feet. "Well, I suppose the only thing is to try to remove it as quickly as possible. Maybe," and a spark of hope stirred in his eyes, "maybe I can get a tugboat to pull it out to sea. Perhaps it won't be so bad."

Mr. Turk studied the overcast sky, glanced out to sea. "Looks sort of squally, Mr. Coves. In fact, there's a storm forecasted. I doubt if you could get a tug to come out here till the weather clears up."

As if to punctuate Mr. Turk's words, a gust of wind blew in from the sea and a great sullen breaker threw a cloud of spume across the beach.

"Maybe the storm will wash the whale to sea."

Mr. Turk snapped his fingers. "Look here, I've got an idea. Carper won't come out if there's a storm. They can't get ashore, even if they wanted to."

Coves hesitated. "But surely the storm won't last more than a day or so."

"By that time maybe Carper's launch will be broke down." He winked. "At least we can tell the guests it's broke down, and there's no way to get ashore. So long as Carper don't call, they won't have any choice but to stay at the hotel."

Coves shook his head decisively. "No, I wouldn't be a party to deception of that sort. And after all we only have supplies for three or four days."

"I think it's worth trying," argued Mr. Turk. "If by some chance we got the whale off the beach, or the storm washed it off, they might even forget the whole matter."

He finally convinced Coves and set off across the hill to Miss Pickett's landing, where Al Carper called before circling around to the hotel. Here he waited till the launch called; by this time the wind was blowing very freshly, and whitecaps flecked the bay. Carper readily agreed to the subterfuge, and Mr. Turk returned to the hotel.

The storm raged in earnest all afternoon and most of the night. About dawn the wind died, and when Coves, in slippers and bathrobe, hurried to the front entrance, the skies were pale and clear as alabaster, and the ocean presented only medium-sized breakers to the beach.

Coves moaned. The whale had been moved a full hundred feet closer to the hotel, and now lay high and dry on the beach.

Coves ventured out on the sand, approaching the whale as closely as the stench allowed. And now he saw coming down the beach the figure of Milo Green.

Milo joined Coves on the windward side of the whale and stood observing the hulk.

"Bad luck, Mr. Coves, bad luck. It seems to dog all of us. Ike, you, me, Miss Pickett, Mr. Ottenbright —"

Coves looked up. "How Mr. Ottenbright?"

"Well," said Milo, "the way I hear it, he brought his stenographer across to catch up on some neglected office work. Archer happened to meet Mrs. Ottenbright in Monterey, and she decided she wanted to join her husband at their house. Archer brought her across, and I hear that a violent scene resulted, after which Mr. Ottenbright sold his property to Archer."

"Too bad," said Coves. "Too bad."

Milo inspected the whale with respect. "What do you propose to do with the carcass?"

Coves shook his head. "I've no idea. I'd pay a thousand dollars to get it off the premises today."

"A thousand dollars?" Milo examined the whale anew.

"A thousand dollars," said Coves firmly, "if you can remove and dispose of the whale."

Milo turned and ran down the beach toward his dock.

Three hours later a helicopter coasted down on Bird Island, the same machine used in the construction of Milo's house. Milo and the pilot jumped out, inspected the project.

"Ought to be able to take it in about four chunks," said the pilot, rolling himself a cigarette. Milo unloaded an axe, a big knife, a gasoline-driven chain saw and a gas mask.

Coves appeared and surveyed the operations with a rueful smile. "Now if I'd thought of that, I'd have saved myself a thousand dollars. Imagination, Mr. Green, it's imagination that counts, and I'm afraid that's where I'm short, especially when my mind's in such a whirl."

Milo said with a grin, "I've sold the carcass to the slaughterhouse for two hundred dollars."

Coves blinked, swallowed. "Well, go to it. Anything you can make out of it you're welcome to, so long as you get it off of my beach."

Stripping to his shorts and donning the gas mask, Milo set to work, while the pilot and Coves watched in frank admiration.

Presently they were joined by others from the hotel.

A half hour passed. From the whale came a muffled shout. Milo emerged clutching a chunk of an oily gray substance the size of his head.

"Ambergris!" The word passed from lip to lip.

"Ambergris!" shouted Milo through the gas mask. "He's full of it!"

"My word!" gasped Coves. "That whale is a gold mine!"

Mr. Turk said, "And to think I turned down a chance to cut myself into that dough."

Coves said manfully, "Well, all I really cared about was getting the whale off the beach. I'm glad Mr. Green was lucky enough to profit."

"That's a quarter free," said Milo. He made the hooks fast, gathered up his sacks of ambergris, carried them to the helicopter.

The pilot said casually, "Just what have you got in mind?"

"I was going to toss the ambergris into the cabin," said Milo. "Then we're ready to take off."

" 'We'?" The pilot drew back an inch or two. "Not in my plane. If you or any other part of that whale rides with this plane, it's on the landing gear."

Milo shouldered the ambergris, stepped off up the hill toward his house.

The 'copter rose, lofted the quarter-whale, swung out over the bay toward Monterey.

CHAPTER XX

THE ACADEMY WAS VACANT. The corridors echoed with silence; the grounds spread bare and lonely.

Tiger Joe sat in the social hall reading a *True Detective Magazine*, lips clenched grimly around a cigarette.

Mortimer Archer pushed open the door, stepped quietly in. He was wearing slacks of a beautiful warm beige, an ivory sports shirt, a brown checked jacket, cordovan shoes.

He looked casually left and right, then sauntered across the room to where Tiger Joe sat.

"I saw your ball and chain going ashore in the launch and thought I'd drop in for a little chat."

"Glad you came," said Tiger Joe. "I need some dough. How about a couple hundred?"

Archer raised his eyebrows. "A couple hundred? What's wrong with the old lady's pocketbook?"

Tiger Joe's face flushed. "Cut the gab and spring some dough."

Archer grinned. "She's bearing down, eh? Well sorry, Joe, but I'm broke. Stone, flat broke."

"Don't give me that stuff, Slippy. You were loaded a few days ago. I saw the wad myself."

"Things have been happening, Joe. I had money this morning. I had money an hour ago. Do you know what I did with that money?"

"Spring it."

"I just bought Ike O'Rourke's place out from under him."

Tiger Joe froze. "You did *what*?"

Archer nodded. "Happened to drop in on him, and he said he was sick of it. Didn't like the climate, the air, the people, the grub. His dogs don't like it, either. So he's packing his baggage, his dogs, his wife, and they're leaving for Alaska tomorrow. I gave him ten thousand cool cash for his property. He was glad to get it."

"I gotta hand it to you, Slippy," breathed Tiger Joe, "you always seem to be in the right place at the right time."

Archer hitched at the crease in his slacks, settled into a chair. "Things are shaping up pretty good. I figure that whale chased off about half Coves' guests."

Tiger Joe curled his lip. "And Green paid off most of his house with what he made on the deal."

"Green's the least of my worries," said Mr. Archer negligently. "Right now I need dough and I need it bad."

"So?"

"So there's going to be an operation tonight."

"Is that right, now?" said Tiger Joe in a restrained voice. "Full scale?"

"Not too big," said Archer. "There's a plane leaving Ensenada this afternoon, and it'll be offshore about eight o'clock. If my figures are correct, the bundle should wash up tomorrow morning about five or six. The cut will be about ten thousand apiece."

Tiger Joe licked his lips. "That part sounds good. The old lady — she's just a little — well, thrifty."

"You'll be rolling in dough after a while," said Archer. "That dance pavilion should make a fortune, if I'm any judge. A perfect setup. Country-club atmosphere, publicity —"

"We already got the picture," said Tiger Joe coolly.

Archer glanced at his wristwatch. "Well, it's six o'clock —"

"Six o'clock?" Tiger Joe glanced out across the bay in the direction of Monterey. "You better get going. Might not look right if we —"

Archer's smile was understanding. "Scared of the old lady, eh? Well, can't say as I blame you. Now listen. I'll meet you by that flagpole at four-thirty tomorrow morning. You got an alarm clock?"

Tiger Joe nodded. "I'll be there."

Mortimer Archer lit a cigarette, strolled out the door. Tiger Joe raised himself to his feet, grunted, muttered under his breath and stamped off to his room.

From a couch across the room Celia arose. She stared after Tiger Joe, then opened the door and fled up the hill toward Milo's house.

Milo listened intently. "What is it they're going to pick up?"

Celia hesitated. "They didn't say. Archer mentioned a 'medium-sized bundle'."

Milo rubbed his chin with the tips of his fingers. "Celia, if this bundle is stolen jewelry, there's sure to be a reward on it. Suppose tomorrow morning I'm down there on the beach, too? If I find the bundle before Archer and Connolly, I'll get the reward and pay off what's left on the house."

Celia said hesitantly, "Won't it be dangerous, Milo? After all, they're criminals."

"What danger could there be? It's right in front of the hotel; they can't pull any rough stuff."

"I don't like it, Milo," said Celia in a troubled voice.

"Now, Celia — here's our chance to make five or ten thousand dollars. The reward will surely be that much."

Celia went to the window. "I'm scared, Milo."

"There's nothing to be scared of," said Milo. "Nothing at all."

She turned. "In that case, I'm coming with you. Then whatever happens to you will happen to us both. No, Milo," and she put her hand over his mouth, "don't argue, because I mean it."

CHAPTER XXI

DAWN CAME CALM, cool, clear to Bird Island. The ocean stretched westward, the water gray, quiet, and the chime of the surf muffled. The sand lay flat and blank.

The sky became pink and pearly behind the island, and colored light seeped around the horizon.

They stood on the edge of Coves' property, just below Milo's house. The beach was empty.

"I guess it's still early," said Milo.

"It's quarter to five," said Celia. "If Mr. Archer met Joe Connolly at four-thirty, they should be here by now."

"Look," said Milo. "There's Archer now, coming down the steps of the hotel."

"But where's Joe Connolly?"

Milo shook his head. "Let's get out there before he finds the stuff himself."

They stepped out of the shadows, advanced down the beach. Archer looked up, froze.

"Hello," sang out Milo. "What are you doing out so early?"

"I might ask the same of you," observed Archer tartly.

"Oh, we come out here often," said Celia. "It's about the only time my aunt isn't keeping an eye on me."

"I see." Archer laughed politely. He turned, looked up and down the shore. "I enjoy the walk myself. This is the loveliest time of day. It gives me a sense of uplift. I especially enjoy the solitude." He emphasized the word. "Of course I don't mind you two as much as I might others." He looked up and down the beach, out to sea.

"What are you looking for?" Celia asked. "More of those little glass bottles?"

Archer darted her a blank stare. "Bottles? Why, no."

Milo walked swiftly down to the water's edge, his eyes on a wooden box floating a hundred feet offshore.

Hearing a sharp voice in the lobby, then a muttered conversation, Coves jumped into his bathrobe, eased open the door and peered through the crack.

He opened it farther, marched out in alarm. "What's all this? What's going on here?"

"Quiet," said Emmett Tharp. He handed Coves a card encased in plastic.

CERTIFICATE OF IDENTIFICATION, read Coves. FEDERAL BUREAU OF INVESTIGATION. The face in the photograph was that of Mr. Emmett Tharp. Coves looked up in consternation, then turned to Tiger Joe, who was seated in a chair, his back turned to the lobby door. "And Mr. Connolly — is he a G-man, too?"

"Mr. Connolly," said Emmett Tharp, "is a notorious criminal recently discharged from San Quentin."

"He ain't got a thing on me," snarled Tiger Joe.

"Unfortunately that is true," said Emmett Tharp. "At the moment. But chances are your confederate will turn state's evidence."

"Confederate?" gasped Coves.

Following Mr. Tharp's gesture, he ran to the window. "Why, it's Mr. Green, and Mr. Archer, and Miss Marlowe. Not all of them?"

"No," said Emmett Tharp. "Probably not."

"But," blurted Coves, "what have they done?"

"Dealing in dope. Smuggling narcotics."

Coves sagged. "How do you know?"

"There's some loose ends, I'll admit," said Mr. Tharp. "But we know that the syndicate has a representative here on Bird Island. At least one, maybe more." He jerked his head toward Tiger Joe. "I'm betting on Joe Connolly.

"We got a tip from Mexico last night that a shipment was on its way. They plan to drop the stuff from a plane, let it float into shore. We've known for months that the gang was using Bird Island for a base, but this will be the first time they've tried to land a shipment."

"Exactly what is the proof for all these accusations?" asked Coves weakly.

Mr. Tharp motioned out on the beach. "See those people out there? One of 'em is waiting for a case of dope to wash ashore. One of 'em posted Joe Connolly here in the lobby for a lookout. Too bad I happened to be laying for 'em. Well, whoever I find in possession of that dope, I'll assume guilty. It stands to reason that the man expecting the dope will make sure he gets it."

"My word," muttered Coves. "It looks like Mr. Green has seen something in the water."

Chapter XXII

"A box," said Celia. "That's funny, isn't it?" She laughed uneasily. "I wonder what it is?"

Archer casually joined Milo at the water's edge. "Oh, probably just a bit of driftwood."

"No," said Celia. "It's a case of some sort. I guess it's yours, Milo, by the laws of flotsam and jetsam."

Archer stood stiffly silent. The case drifted closer to the beach, rose and fell on the swells.

Archer made a forward movement, restrained himself. He said, "I say, Green, let's be sporting about that crate. As I see it, we're both here and both have an equal right to it. Might even be valuable." He laughed awkwardly. "Let's flip a coin for it."

"No," said Milo with a grin. "Thanks just the same. I'll retain my original right of discovery. At least until I see what it is."

The crate reached the line of breaking surf, rose, fell back, rose again, caught in the tumble of foam, came rushing in to shore. Milo stepped forward. Archer stumbled against him and Milo fell face down into the surf.

"Sorry, old man," said Archer. "Sorry indeed."

Milo rose to his feet, dripping. Archer held the crate. Milo stepped forward and hit Archer on the jaw. Archer tottered back, reached into his hip pocket with his free hand. Milo jumped forward, hit him again, and Archer fell to his knees in the sand. A small automatic was in his hand. Milo drove at him, put a knee into his neck, knocked the gun twenty feet away, where Celia pounced on it. For a moment he struggled for the box, finally wrested it free.

He stood back panting, then turned his gaze to the box.

From the hotel there came the sound of footsteps.

"Mr. Green," said Emmett Tharp, "consider yourself under arrest."

"Arrest!" shouted Milo. "For what? And just who the hell are you?"

"FBI," said Emmett Tharp. "You're under arrest for running dope."

"Dope?"

"I've suspected it all along," chimed in Archer.

Milo turned his gaze down on the wooden case. "This isn't dope. This is —"

"Is what, Mr. Green?"

"I don't know."

"Open it and see," suggested Celia.

"Dope," whispered Milo. "My God."

Coves came forward with a rock and began to pound on the case.

"I'm afraid you're in serious trouble, Mr. Green," said Emmett Tharp. "Why don't you come clean and turn state's evidence?"

"But I haven't done anything!"

"You're in possession of a case of dope. You attacked Mr. Archer to prevent him from inspecting it. I saw it myself —"

"An unprovoked assault," declared Archer. "An outrage. Good work, Captain."

Emmett Tharp nodded complaisantly.

"You'll have to come along with me, Mr. Green."

"You're crazy!" roared Milo. "Just because I pick up a crate on the beach —"

"Why are you out here at five in the morning to meet it, then?" asked Emmett Tharp.

A cracking sound came from the crate. He turned. "Careful, Mr. Coves, that's evidence."

Coves pulled away the lid, exposing a number of water-logged cardboard packages. Emmett Tharp pulled out one of these, and the cardboard slid off in a gray slush. He held a toy battleship of red celluloid. He squinted at the bottom. "Made in Japan."

He shook it. No sound. He opened another carton. A red celluloid battleship. Made in Japan.

"My word," said Coves, "these must have floated clear across the Pacific."

"Hmmph," snorted Milo. "Dope."

"Ahem," said Emmett Tharp. "I guess I haven't got the goods on you after all."

"If you'll listen to me," said Celia furiously, "I'll tell you exactly why we happened to come out here this morning."

A wooden box similar in appearance to the first slid up on the beach in a smother of foam.

The group looked at it as if it were a bomb. No one moved.

Celia said resolutely, "Yesterday afternoon in the main hall at the academy, I woke up from a nap —"

Archer edged away, sauntered down the beach, gradually lengthened his stride.

"This morning Milo and I came out to see just what was going on —"

Archer climbed the slope of the hill, approached the saddle.

"Then you arrested Milo, and now Mr. Archer has gone, and you've botched everything."

Mr. Tharp shook his head. "I'd hardly say that, young lady."

"Suppose Mr. Archer gets ashore and escapes?"

"Slippy Archer doesn't stand a chance of escaping."

"Just what do you mean?"

Mr. Tharp shook his head with a smile. "Sorry, I can't say anything more."

"How about Mr. Connolly?" inquired Coves. "The indications seem to be that he is equally involved in this crime."

"True," said Emmett Tharp. "True." He frowned. "Of course, by the very nature of this case, there is even less evidence against Joe Connolly than against Mortimer Archer. In any event, Joe Connolly will endure — that is, will be guided by his wife; and, though I hesitate to control the workings of justice, in this case I'm rather inclined to let fate, destiny, retribution — whatever you want to call it — take its own course." He glanced at the second box. "And now, Mr. Coves, if you'll hand me that rock, we'll see what's what."

Mortimer Archer returned to his house with nervous steps. Pack up and leave — things were getting too hot. Lucky for him that events had turned out as they had. "Curse the luck," muttered Archer.

He pushed his key into the lock, froze. The door was ajar.

Archer pushed the door slowly open, peered within.

A man sat in his chair, smoking a cigarette. To Archer's trained perceptions the man carried about him an unmistakable aura.

The man said, "Come on in, Archer; come on in."

Archer stalked in. "What's the meaning of this intrusion? Who the devil are you, sir?"

The man reached into his breast pocket, came out with a folded piece of paper. He tapped it against his thumb.

"This is a search warrant." He tendered it to Archer, who waved it away. The man handed him another piece of paper. "And this is a warrant for your arrest."

"Arrest?" blustered Archer. "On what grounds?"

"Sending pornographic material through the mails."

"Are you crazy?"

"No." The man rose to his feet. "Quit your kidding, Slippy. The innocent act is just plain foolish."

Archer said quickly, "If you're narrow-minded enough to consider artistic photographs pornography — I'd like to make it clear that I have never used the mail, but always express."

The other man smiled. "They've gone out from Monterey by express."

"Well?"

"How did they get to Monterey?"

"Why…" Mr. Archer considered. "Sometimes I'd take them in myself, sometimes a friend dropped them off."

"And who was the friend?"

Archer's jaw dropped. "Why — none of your business."

"It was Al Carper."

Mr. Archer said nothing.

"Al Carper," said the plain-clothes man, "is an employee of the United States Post Office. Better get together what you're going to need."

Milo and Celia walked up the beach, each thinking his own thoughts.

The incident on the beach had not ended on a plane of effusive cordiality. Mr. Tharp had been annoyed to find that the second case contained battleships of green celluloid. Coves had been petulant at what he termed Mr. Tharp's 'scare tactics'.

They climbed the hill, and hand in hand entered Milo's house of stone and glass and redwood. The sun shone full in the windows and flooded the house with the molten gold of morning.

"Speaking of marriage, today is the third day of the waiting period, and we can be married. Right now."

"Where'll we go on our honeymoon, Milo?"

Milo squinted thoughtfully. "I hadn't considered."

Celia went to the window. To the south, the dark headlands of Point Lobos, Carmel, Pebble Beach. To the north, the misty shoreline of Monterey Bay. To the west the ineffable reaches of the Pacific, sun-drenched and blue.

"We could stay right here, Milo," said Celia. "Especially since neither one of us has any money. When you're a famous author, we'll take a trip around the world."

"Darling," said Milo.

Rexie, happening by a few minutes later, chanced to glance in the window. He met Milo's eyes over Celia's shoulder. Milo winked broadly. Rexie stared inscrutably a moment; then continued on his way toward the hotel.

Jack Vance was born in 1916 to a well-off California family that, as his childhood ended, fell upon hard times. As a young man he worked at a series of unsatisfying jobs before studying mining engineering, physics, journalism and English at the University of California Berkeley. Leaving school as America was going to war, he found a place as an ordinary seaman in the merchant marine. Later he worked as a rigger, surveyor, ceramicist, and carpenter before his steady production of sf, mystery novels, and short stories established him as a full-time writer.

His output over more than sixty years was prodigious and won him three Hugo Awards, a Nebula Award, a World Fantasy Award for lifetime achievement, as well as an Edgar from the Mystery Writers of America. The Science Fiction and Fantasy Writers of America named him a grandmaster and he was inducted into the Science Fiction Hall of Fame.

His works crossed genre boundaries, from dark fantasies (including the highly influential *Dying Earth* cycle of novels) to interstellar space operas, from heroic fantasy (the *Lyonesse* trilogy) to murder mysteries featuring a sheriff (the Joe Bain novels) in a rural California county. A Vance story often centered on a competent male protagonist thrust into a dangerous, evolving situation on a planet where adventure was his daily fare, or featured a young person setting out on a perilous odyssey over difficult terrain populated by entrenched, scheming enemies.

Late in his life, a world-spanning assemblage of Vance aficionados came together to return his works to their original form, restoring material cut by editors whose chief preoccupation was the page count of a pulp magazine. The result was the complete and authoritative *Vance Integral Edition* in 44 hardcover volumes. Spatterlight Press is now publishing the VIE texts as ebooks, and as print-on-demand paperbacks.

Colophon

This book was printed using Adobe Arno Pro as the primary text font, with NeutraFace used on the cover.

This title was created from the digital archive of the Vance Integral Edition, a series of 44 books produced under the aegis of the author by a worldwide group of his readers. The VIE project gratefully acknowledges the editorial guidance of Norma Vance, as well as the cooperation of the Department of Special Collections at Boston University, whose John Holbrook Vance collection has been an important source of textual evidence.

Special thanks to R.C. Lacovara, Patrick Dusoulier, Koen Vyverman, Paul Rhoads, Chuck King, Gregory Hansen, Suan Yong, and Josh Geller for their invaluable assistance preparing final versions of the source files.

Digitize: Richard Chandler, Joel Hedlund, Andreas Irle, John A. Schwab; Format: R.C. Lacovara; Diff: David Reitsema, Dave Worden; Tech Proof: Dave Worden; Text Integrity: Paul Rhoads, Steve Sherman, Dave Worden; Implement: Derek W. Benson, Mike Dennison; Security: Paul Rhoads; Compose: Andreas Irle; Comp Review: Christian J. Corley, Charles King, Paul Rhoads, Robin L. Rouch; Update Verify: Marcel van Genderen, Charles King, Paul Rhoads, Robin L. Rouch, Dave Worden; RTF-Diff: Errico Rescigno, Textport: Patrick Dusoulier; Proofread: Marc Herant, Karl Kellar, David A. Kennedy, Bob Luckin, Robert Melson, Jim Pattison, Joel Riedesel, Robin L. Rouch, Hans van der Veeke, Douglas Wilson

Artwork (maps based on original drawings by Jack and Norma Vance):

Paul Rhoads, Christopher Wood

Book Composition and Typesetting: Joel Anderson

Art Direction and Cover Design: Howard Kistler

Proofing: Steve Sherman, Dave Worden

Jacket Blurb: Patrick Dusoulier, Steve Sherman, John Vance

Management: John Vance, Koen Vyverman